I0570753

PREVIOUS PRAISE FOR NATHAN TUCKER

JULIA'S

CHRISTMAS

CAROL

NATHAN W. TUCKER

InArena Publishing House

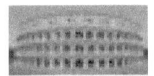

Julia's Christmas Carol is a work of fiction. Names, characters, places, and incidents are the products of the author's imagination or are used fictitiously. Any resemblance to actual events, locales, or persons, living or dead, is entirely coincidental.

ISBN: 0615886868
ISBN-13: 978-0615886862

InArena Publishing House

Dedicated to the redemption of Julia's everywhere.

The Forgotten Man

The type and formula of most schemes of philanthropy or humanitarianism is this: A and B put their heads together to decide what C shall be made to do for D. The radical vice of all these schemes, from a sociological point of view, is that C is not allowed a voice in the matter, and his position, character, and interests, as well as the ultimate effects on society through C's interests, are entirely overlooked. I call C the Forgotten Man...

The friends of humanity start out with certain benevolent feelings toward "the poor," "the weak," "the laborers," and others of whom they make pets. They generalize these classes, and render them impersonal, and so constitute the classes into social pets...

They are always under the dominion of the superstition of government, and, forgetting that a government produces nothing at all, they leave out of sight the first fact to be remembered in all social discussion—that the state cannot get a cent for any man without taking it from some other man, and this latter must be a man who has produced and saved it. This latter is the Forgotten Man...

—William Graham Sumner (1883)

STAVE ONE.

MARLEE'S GHOST

Marlee was dead, having quietly left this life for the next as she slept in Yuletide slumber last Christmas Eve. Her death from a massive heart attack was shocking to those who knew her for, though forty, she had been the model of perfect health.

She was a health fanatic—running marathons, competing in triathlons, maintaining a perfect diet, and never, ever, indulging in sweets. Her health was the most important thing to her, leaving little room in her life for anything, or anyone, else.

It wasn't that she didn't love people. Quite the opposite, she loved people so much that she became a crusader of various causes for the advancement of humanity. She cared for the needy, so she advocated for government-run welfare programs. She wished that everyone could be as healthy as she was, so she promoted government-run health insurance.

She was concerned with those who had lost jobs, so she wanted the government to do more to create jobs. She empathized with the victims of violence, so she urged stricter gun laws. She feared that environmental pollution was destroying the earth for future generations, so she fought for great environmental regulations.

But despite all this compassion, she never deigned to actually help another human being in need. Instead of giving to individuals or private charities, Marlee reserved her time and money for political candidates and parties. Only government, she was convinced, could save humanity from itself. For her, caring for others meant controlling them through government coercion.

Upon her passing, however, the government was too busy running other people's lives to pause and pay its respects at her funeral. Only a handful of friends and colleagues managed to attend the service, while others spared just enough time to send cards and flowers. Though a few politicians and activists sent flattering notes of condolences, most simply used the occasion to push for even more government measures designed to ensure the early detection of heart disease in women.

Those who knew her loved her, but they were sadly in short supply. Between her political causes and her budding career as a website designer, she never found the time to marry or have children. It wasn't that she didn't want to eventually have a family, there just was never a good time for her to do so. Unbeknownst to her, that opportunity would never come, for the sands of time, with their usual sudden abruptness, had escaped the hourglass of her life.

Today marked the first anniversary of her passing, and only her business partner Julia remembered the solemn occasion. She usually made it a point to avoid cemeteries, fearing the specter of death that haunts every tombstone and mausoleum. This morning, however, she found herself strangely compelled to visit Marlee's gravesite before she headed to work.

Now as she laid a wreath of Christmas poinsettias by the tombstone, Julia sought to keep her gaze solely on her friend's final resting place. Desiring to avoid the reminder of her own mortality, she wished to avoid seeing the rows upon rows of dead around her. Though she knew that she would inevitably join them, she hoped, with the aid of government medicine and nannyism, to keep that fatal day in the far distant future.

Standing there, Julia felt ashamed that no one else had bothered to place flowers by Marlee's grave. They should pass a law, she thought, that required cemeteries to place flowers at every tombstone, for it was unfair that some should have flowers while others do not. Besides, it was expecting too much for family and friends to take precious time out of their busy lives to visit the dead.

As she was mentally adding this idea to her to-do list, the nature of Marlee's untimely death suddenly reminded Julia that she had forgotten to get her annual health exam. Another item was added to her legislative agenda—requiring doctors to send out notices to patients to get annual exams. Like her late partner, Julia was fond of thinking of ways that government could improve people's lives. After all, she reminded herself, humans are frail and imperfect beings that need the government like a child needs a parent.

Though she was like Marlee in many ways, she was hardly a health nut. Instead of exercising, she was always trying new "lose weight now" shakes, pills, and exercise-free gadgets like that belt that was supposed to give her abs of steel while sitting on the couch. When each eventually failed, she would proceed to file multiple complaints with the FDA, the Consumer Protection Agency, the Better Business Bureau, and to lobby for yet more government regulations and oversight.

Never once did she consider darkening the door of a gym or watching what she ate. She had a sweet tooth and never refrained from indulging it. Instead of taking responsibility for her actions, she trusted that the government could erase the consequences of her personal failings. Life was hard enough as it was, she rationalized, without the constant burden of stewardship and inner discipline.

Still a strikingly beautiful woman at the age of thirty-nine, she could easily have any man she desired. But the problem is that she never desired a romantic relationship, or at least that's what she kept telling herself. She felt that it was beneath her feminist ideals to make someone other than herself the love of her life. Besides, she reasoned, her schedule simply didn't allow for a time-consuming and emotionally draining dating life.

But staring at Marlee's forsaken and unadorned tombstone, a pang of loneliness and fear slowly crept over her as she wondered who, if anyone, would visit her own grave upon her passing. She could think of one, maybe two dozen friends, employees, and acquaintances who might show up at her funeral, but she couldn't think of a single person who would return to her gravesite once she was in the ground. She was Marlee's closest friend, and she hadn't planned this visit, nor did she anticipate making any new ones in the future.

Perhaps, she thought, she could ensure her fond remembrance by having a child. She grimaced, though, at the prospect of messing with sperm donors or actually going through nine-months of pregnancy followed by the painful throes of child birth. And the thought of the sleepless nights carrying for a baby by herself nearly drove the notion completely from the realm of possibility.

But then her eyes quickly brightened as she imagined adopting an orphaned child. Not an infant; too much hassle. It would need to be old enough to do many things on its own, but not too old that it was already an insolent adolescent. And of course it would need to be a boy—cheaper and not as high maintenance as a girl.

Even as she made her way out of the cemetery past the markers of the long-forgotten dead, Julia smiled as she day-dreamed of the designer adoptive son that would always carry her in his heart. Lost in thoughts of her imaginary son's ideal weight, height, gene pool, intelligence, and the monument he will place—and visit— at her gravesite, she almost didn't hear the street beggar cry out to her as she reached the street.

"Could you spare a dollar or two, miss, during this season of giving?" the vagabond asked again as he held out an eager palm in desperate expectation. "I lost my job, and my family will have neither food nor heat this Christmas."

Unhappy that her blissful reverie was so rudely interrupted, Julia paused and cast a cool eye upon the miserable, unfortunate man. Usually she would simply ignore beggars and continue on her way, but this man wasn't the typical unwashed, uncouth, alcoholic vagrant she usually saw on the streets. Carrying himself with a natural self-assurance, he was clean shaven and sober and looked like he could be any average doctor, lawyer, or businessman.

But rather than pity him for whatever misfortune had befallen him, she found herself overcome with rage at his audacity to ask for yet more charity.

"Sir," she asked in a measured, stern voice that belied her seething anger, "have I not already given enough? Have I not been taxed enough to provide you with numerous government aid programs? Or has the unemployment fund run dry? Or that for worker's compensation? Or social security disability? Or food stamps? Or Medicaid? Or government housing?"

"You ungrateful, impertinent wretch," she continued, her words now dripping with guile. "I have already given you ample charity, and you shall not get a cent more. If you're still destitute after all I've done for you, it's your own fault."

And with that, Julia abruptly turned to continue down the sidewalk towards her office. The beggar, bewildered but uncowed, called after her, "Thank you, but ma'am, true compassion is an attitude of the heart, not an act of self-righteousness. 'If I give all I possess to the poor but do not have love, I gain nothing. Love does not boast, it is not proud, it is not self-seeking.'"[1]

His words pierced Julia's conscience, momentarily stopping her haughty march towards the seclusion of her office building. She recalled hearing the passage before, but found herself unable to remember where.

As much as she hated to do so, curiosity prompted her to turn around to ask the slacker

[1] I Corinthians 13 (NIV)

about the phrase and its meaning. But he wasn't there. She looked up and down the street, but he was nowhere to be seen. Good riddance, she thought, he's probably on his way to his favorite bar to begin his long overdue start on drinking for the day.

His words, however, continued to trouble her as she made her way through the town square towards her office, but she was largely successful in convincing herself they were the ramblings of a drunken fool. She tried to distract herself by cursing the overdecorated town square that would make the Whos of Dr. Seuss' Whoville green with envy.

Every tree in the square was decorated with care, adorned so that not a single inch was bare. A giant evergreen graced the center of the scene, a gift from the glad heart of Georgine. At its base lay the manager in its place, while nearby carolers sang with such grace. And across the way she saw the children in play, waiting for a chance to ride the sleigh.

But none of this cheered Julia's heart, which with age had grown cold and dark. It wasn't that she was a Grinch, for she had no desire to deprive others of their joy. But she was an atheist or, at best, an agnostic who believed that the existence of God was unknowable. Not that she had ever bothered to try to find God for herself, for she was too busy pretending to be the master of her own life.

But by refusing to make room for the Divine in her heart, Julia came to despise the Christmas holiday for, despite all of its commercialized trappings, it remained at heart the celebration of the birth of the Incarnate—God made flesh to redeem us. *Bah humbug!*[2] Julia silently muttered to herself as she once again recoiled at the notion that she needed saving. She was a self-made woman, she assured herself, who had no need to be saved by either a deity or a man.

"Bah humbug!" she muttered again, this time out loud as she found herself becoming incensed over the Christ in Christmas.

"Excuse me, ma'am?"   asked the bemused deliveryman as he stood opening the door for her to enter her building. Her office occupied the top floor of a two-story colonial brick building that matched most of the others that surrounded the square. Only city hall, the courthouse, and the library were allowed to deviate from this architectural code. Though built over a century ago, the building was well maintained and installed with all the latest modern conveniences.

"Thank you," Julia managed as she quickly walked past him in embarrassment.   She had

---

[2] To refer to something as a "humbug" is to call it a fraud or deceit.

noticed that she was developing a bad habit of talking out loud in public, and cautioned herself to be more aware of her surroundings.

"You're welcome," chuckled the deliveryman, "and have a very merry Christmas!"

"And many happy holidays to you as well," Julia replied as he walked out the door to resume his route. She hated even using the word *Christmas*, making a deliberate effort to use the more generic *Happy Holidays* whenever she could.

She glanced at her watch as she mounted the stairs. 9:30 a.m. Two hours later than she usually arrived at work. She was a workaholic—preferring to be the first one in the office in the morning and the last one to leave in the evening, often staying until 8 or 9 at night.

She expected the same commitment from her associates, which is why they never lasted that long. On average they only stayed nine months, with the record of three years held by an associate who ended his streak by hanging himself upon learning that he would not make partner. Only Marlee could match her time commitment hour for hour, a manic work ethic that helped the two partners create one of the most successful website design companies in the region.

"Good morning, Julia!" greeted Mary, the receptionist, when she entered the office. There would be no *Merry Christmas!* here, nor even a *Happy Holidays!* if it could be avoided without giving offense. The only decorations allowed were generic seasonal snow scenes, with nary a tinsel nor a light nor a manger scene in sight.

The only concession she made to the holiday was to give her employees Christmas Day off with pay. Julia and Marlee had experimented with refusing such a concession when they first started out, but they quickly found it difficult to keep qualified employees without at least giving them Christmas off. Most had enough vacation time, scarce though it was, that this year all the employees save Mary had taken Christmas Eve off as well.

Try as she might, Julia struggled to accomplish much of anything in the office. She was planning on working on Christmas Day as well, and had hoped to use the peace and quite of an empty office to finish a large project that was due at the end of the year. But despite the looming deadline, Julia spent the day loathing Christmas, interspersed occasionally with daydreams of her designer adoptive son.

"Good night, Julia!" Mary said, standing in the doorway to Julia's office as she struggled to put her coat on.

"Good night?" Julia asked, startled out of her daydream. Glancing at the clock on the wall, Julia was shocked to find that it was already five in the afternoon. Chagrined at her procrastination, she wondered how she had let an entire day go by without doing a single thing.

"I'll be here bright and early the day after tomorrow," Mary continued.

"Thank you," Julia replied. "Enjoy the time with your family."

"You know you're always welcome to join us for dinner," Mary said hopefully, concerned with her boss's self-imposed isolation. At least in years past Marlee always worked with Julia on Christmas, but now the thought of Julia alone in her office troubled the long-serving secretary. She had been with them since the beginning, outlasting the associates because at least she had set office hours.

"What are you having?" Julia inquired, temporarily tempted by the allure of a home-cooked meal. She loved home-cooking, just not enough to actually cook it herself. She lived mostly on takeout and fast-food, unwilling to spare time from work to make her own food.

"We're having honey-coated spiral ham, mashed potatoes, stuffing, corn casserole, rolls, fruit salads, vegetable salads, and birthday cake for dessert."

"Birthday cake?" Julia asked, unaware that anyone in Mary's family had a Christmas birthday.

"Jesus' birthday cake, of course," Mary replied, trying her best to appear calm while every second expecting an angry outburst.

"Then you know I can't join you," Julia said painfully, looking as if she had just been slapped. She had actually started to look forward to dinner with Mary's family, but the reminder of its religious nature shocked her back to reality. It'll just be leftover Chinese food for her tomorrow.

"I know," said Mary dejectedly, and, after warning her boss not to work too hard, she left to go home to her family.

After stewing for another thirty minutes on how much she hated Christmas, Julia finally gave up hope of doing anything productive and called it a day. There was always tomorrow, after all, to work on the project. Besides, she was hungry with all the talk of food and wanted to stop at the family diner on the way home. It wasn't quite home-cooking, but it'll do.

After eating and with leftovers in hand, Julia left the diner and in the dark nearly collided with a lonely bell ringer who sat with his donation bucket beside him.

"Excuse me!" she exclaimed as she fought to regain her balance.

"I'm sorry, miss," the bell ringer apologized. "I guess I shouldn't have sat so close to the door."

"Why are you still working? It's Christmas Eve and almost no one is about."

"Charity never sleeps, ma'am. Especially when we're still so short of our goal. If we don't reach it by the end of the year, it'll mean layoffs and cutbacks and a lot less good cheer."

"I've never understood the need for private charity," Julia declared emphatically. "All that money should be given to government charity programs. It would be far better to strengthen government welfare rather than to try to duplicate it. Plus, you could get your same job with the government, only with better pay and benefits."

"But ma'am," the bell ringer replied, deeply disturbed at such sophistry, "government charity is coerced charity. It is the forceful taking of what belongs to A in order to give to B. Such coerced charity is no charity at all, but simply robbery sanctioned by the law. It would be far better for both the giver and the receiver if $10 were given willingly than if $100 were taken by force."

Julia stood there mute and perplexed, unable or unwilling to understand what she had just heard. As the bell ringer turned to stroll down the street in search of more generous hearts, the words quoted by the street beggar that morning came suddenly to her mind: *If I give all I possess to the poor but do not have love, I gain nothing. Love does not boast, it is not proud, it is not self-seeking.*

Troubled, Julia quickly made her way to her house a few blocks away. As she turned onto her street, she paused in mid-stride as she spied a group of carolers entertaining the house next to hers. Overcome with fear that they might accost her with their merriment just short of her sanctuary, she suddenly broke into a run as she made for her front door.

Nearly successful, she struggled to find the right key as the carolers moved towards her on the front walk. Finding it just as they began *Silent Night*, she shouted "Bah humbug!" and slammed the door in their bewildered faces. As relief flooded over her, Julia slid down the door and sat in the dark until the nomadic jubilation could be heard no more.

Good grief, Julia thought to herself, thinking that perhaps she should become a hermit during December. Maybe she could work from an isolated log cabin far removed from any reminder of Christmas. Sighing, she looked up and saw in the moonlight a picture of her and Marlee that hung on the wall.

Mystified, Julia looked at it closer. The picture was of the grand opening of their business, and both of them were proudly wielding a giant pair of scissors as they cut the red ribbon. At least, that is how she remembered the picture from walking by it thousands of times before.

Now, however, Marlee's face was animated, lifelike, and staring directly at her as she sat by the door. Her blond hair was blowing in the wind, and her mouth formed words though no sound was heard. She bore an expression of agitation, even fearfulness, as if she were the one haunted rather than the one haunting.

Terrified, Julia jumped to her feet and switched on the entryway light before she cautiously approached the picture for a better look. But to both her comfort and dismay, the picture appeared just as it always had—lifeless and still. It was once more a simple snapshot in time in which she and Marlee had ignored the camera as they focused on the task at hand.

Julia was not given to superstition or a belief in the supernatural, but she knew what she saw and what she saw was not natural. She walked hesitantly in a half-circle by the picture, half expecting Marlee to turn and follow her movements. Unsatisfied when nothing happened, she took the picture off the wall in hopes of finding that it had somehow been programed to come to life. Nothing.

Still not persuaded that the picture was just a picture and nothing more, Julia placed it face-down on the entryway table and tentatively backed away as she looked for any sign of trouble. Nothing happened. Humbug, she thought, as she left to put the leftovers in the kitchen.

She was back in less than a minute, staring intently at the picture for any indication that it had moved in her absence. There was none. It was nothing, she sought to assure herself, just the moonlight playing tricks with her imagination. Still, despite her protestations of confidence, her hands shook nervously as she reached to place the picture back on the wall.

"Julia!" came the haunting, solemn tone of Marlee's voice coming from the picture. This time there could be no denying what she saw as she observed a living, breathing Marlee staring back at her with piercing blue eyes and hand raised accusingly.

Julia shrieked in terror. She rushed to the front door, opened it, and smashed the picture on her front stoop, breaking the frame into thousands of tiny pieces. She slammed the door, locked it, and barricaded it with the heavy oak entryway table.

Still convulsing with fear but fueled by adrenaline, Julia commenced a room by room search for any sign of mischief. Turning on the lights as she went, Julia double-checked the doors and windows while exploring every crook and cranny for any sign of ghosts.

Finding nothing amiss, she retired to the second floor master suite and locked the door, propping a chair under the handle as an extra precaution. She sat despondently in her chair by the fireplace, cradling her head in her hands and mumbling "humbug!" over and over again.

She wished she owned a gun. Perhaps one of those scary looking assault weapons, or at least a shotgun. Maybe they couldn't harm a ghost, but at least they would give her confidence and calm her nerves. But, alas, she hated guns and didn't think that anyone should be allowed to own one. Until now.

Maybe she should contact an exorcist, Julia mused, though she quickly dismissed the notion, convinced that he would think her crazy and seek to have her committed. But perhaps she should see a psychiatrist or a therapist of some kind, someone she could talk to about her issues.

Issues? What issues? She found the thought hilarious and actually doubled-over in laughter despite the fear she still felt. She was a loving, caring, hardworking, self-made woman who had no issues. At least, none serious enough to see a shrink about.

Her narcissism partially restored, Julia crawled into bed determined to have happy dreams about her ideal adoptive child. The events of the evening, she determined, were caused by her dinner and nothing more. She made a mental note to throw out the leftovers in the morning, not wishing to experience another episode like this one.

Just as she was about to drift off to sleep, the bells of the church the next block over began to ring obnoxiously. Odd, she thought, they've never rung at night before. They were soon joined by those of the church several streets over, followed by the church next to the diner, than the church across the square from her office. Soon all the bells in all the town's churches were joined together in clamorous melody.

But just as quickly as they started they fell quite once again. A minute passed, then two, but the foreboding silence only grew as Julia lay terrified in her bed. The stillness of the night was suddenly broken by the sound of heavy chains being dragged on the first floor of the house.

Slowly, as if with great effort, the phantom noise climbed the stairs and approached her bedroom door. "Humbug!" Julia kept muttering over and over again as the clanking increased in volume as the chains neared their unmistakable destination.

She pulled the bedcovers over her head, willing away whatever presence awaited outside her door. Then suddenly it was in her room, chains and all, and stood looming at the foot of her bed.

"Julia!" came the same haunting, solemn voice that had spoken to her from the picture a short time before. Julia knew it was Marlee, but the realization brought little comfort. The ghosts of friends don't pay random visits to the living just to catch up over tea and crumpets.

"Julia!" came the voice again, now with just a hint of impatience. Reluctantly, fearfully, Julia pulled the covers down so that only her eyes were peering over the top. Standing before her was the undeniable figure of Marlee, clothed in the pajamas she had died in last Christmas Eve.

A massive chain was bound around Marlee's waist, the train of which trailed behind her for some length. Whenever it moved, a faint weeping appeared to be coming from its midst. Gazing transfixed upon it, Julia noticed a name written on each link. Hundreds of names held Marlee captive, each one vying with muffled voice to tell its own tale of sorrow.

"May I have a seat?" the Ghost asked, looking winded and tired from her journey up the stairs.

"Please," said Julia, indicating her chair by the fireplace. With great difficulty the Ghost moved to the chair, each step seemingly a feat of monumental strength as she pulled her bonds behind her. And with each clank of the chain a chorus of cries clamored from the shackles, causing the specter's face to contort in compunction and contrition.

"Who are you?" Julia finally managed to ask. She knew, of course, but had no desire to ask the next obvious question, "Why are you here?"

The Ghost chucked ominously. "You know who I am. I am Marlee, your former business partner and friend."

The Ghost just sat there, resting, staring at Julia with unyielding, penetrating eyes. Julia, beginning to tremble, felt as though her soul was naked and exposed to the piercing gaze of the apparition in front of her. Desperate to rid herself of this intimate examination, she found herself clumsily inquiring about the manacles.

"Do you like them?" the Ghost responded.

"No," Julia replied, trying to give as little offense as possible.

"But you must," the Ghost chided her, "for yours is even longer than mine."

"I am afraid that you are mistaken, for I carry no such chain around my person," Julia insisted, grasping for her waist to confirm that no such spectacle imprisoned her.

"It is as real as I am," the Ghost solemnly replied. "You do not see it yet, but it is there, waiting to bind you for all eternity."

"What do the names represent?"

"The people that I have harmed in life. The people that I have stolen from and wronged."

"Stolen?" Julia asked incredulously. "I never saw you steal or hurt anyone in your life. And if you are really Marlee, than you would know the same about me."

"I once thought as you did," the Ghost acknowledged. "In life I suspected they existed, though I refused to see the pain I was causing. But now," she paused, glancing with haunted eyes at her bindings, "I can no longer ignore their names or their stories. They haunt me without end, their cries and their agony never ceasing. But you, my friend, will have a chance to see your victims and, perhaps, unmake the chain that binds you."

Overcome by fear, Julia began shaking uncontrollably though buried deep under her bedding. "Leave me!" she cried, "and go back to the world from whence you came."

"I will," the Ghost said as she slowly rose from the chair. "But tonight you will have the chance of redemption. You will be visited by three spirits who will show you the victims that make up the links of your chain. Look for the first at midnight, followed by the second at one and the last at two."

"I'm sorry," Julia cried as the Ghost struggled towards the bedroom door. "Please stay. One visit is enough. You can tell me what I need to know."

But the Ghost, dragging her chain of sin behind her, no longer paid Julia any attention as she plodded toward the hall.

"Please!" Julia begged. "Please stay. Or, at least, could you send only one spirit? Or perhaps all the spirits at once?"

The questions were greeted only by silence, for with one final lurch the Ghost passed through the door and back into eternity. Warily, Julia got up and placed her ear to the door as she listened intently for any movement on the other side. Hearing none, Julia examined the door and found it still locked and blocked by the chair.

Baffled, Julia made her way back to bed. She didn't have any real expectation of rest, but hoped the warmth would bring an end to her shaking. Remarkably, however, weariness and exhaustion overcame her and she was soon fast asleep.

It was an hour before midnight.

STAVE TWO.

THE GHOST OF CHRISTMAS PAST

Julia woke with a start. She could hear the church bells ringing again, but this time in somber unison. Deep, melancholy notes rolled out across the dark, still town. Three. Four. Five times they rang. Confused, she glanced at her clock. 12:00 midnight.

"No!" Julia screamed, recoiling in horror as the bells continued to toil. She sprang out of bed and grabbed the fireplace poker, brandishing it widely as she turned to survey her empty room.

Eight. Nine. Ten times the bells kept ringing. Seeing no one with her, she ran to the bedroom door and found it just as she had left it. Cupping her ear once again to its side, she strained to hear if any creature was stirring. Nothing.

The bells rang the twelfth time and then fell silent. No one appeared. Slightly disappointed in spite of herself, Julia ran to the window that overlooked the street in hopes of spying a midnight visitor. But the street was empty of any pedestrians, either natural or unearthly.

Forlorn and perplexed, Julia stood there wondering if the entire night had been merely a dream. She began to doubt that she had ever seen

Marlee's ghost, convincing herself once again that it was a dinner-induced hallucination. Maybe that poor, misguided bell ringer had done something with her food.

But just as she was about to leave the window and go back to bed, Julia spied an old man turning the corner onto her street. His hair was long and white, as was his beard which fell to his waist. He was clothed in a frayed and worn cloak; his feet bare and exposed to the elements.

Though from this distance he appeared to be at least a hundred, the man moved with the grace of one unencumbered by age. His stride and his posture were that of a man just shy of twenty, belying his need for the staff he held in his hand. As he turned onto her front walk, Julia could hear his clear, young voice softly singing *Silent Night*.

Suddenly he stopped and looked up at her with a face seemingly no older than adolescence. His skin was smooth and young, with just a hint of recent acne. And despite his white crown, not a wrinkle nor laugh line had ever set foot upon his features. In a miraculous blending of time, he appeared to be both sixteen and one hundred at the same time.

When he smiled at her, she could see a dimple adorning each of his ruddy, freckled checks. His youthful countenance, however, was contradicted by his solemn, ancient eyes that seemed to be deep pools of vast wisdom born of experiences ages past.

"Good Evening!" he greeted, "I have an appointment with you tonight." And with that he walked through her front door.

Julia, still wielding the fireplace poker, could hear his light footsteps as the Spirit made its way up her stairs. Feeling foolish at her cowardice, she flung the weapon across the room where it embedded itself in the wall. She briefly toyed with the idea of opening the door for her guest but, sensing that he had nearly arrived, felt her courage flee her and she hid once more under her blankets.

Then he was in the room. She could hear him walking to the foot of her bed and stopping, saying nothing. She tried not to breathe or move a muscle, hoping to avoid detection by whatever presence awaited her. Why, she thought, did this have to happen to her? Why did she have to eat at the diner tonight?

Marlee's words suddenly intruded upon her self-pitying: "But tonight you will have the chance of redemption." Redemption, scoffed Julia. She didn't need any redemption. She hadn't wronged anyone or taken what wasn't hers. Bah—

"Julia," the Spirit interrupted her before she could finish, "I am no humbug. Arise, for the appointed hour is upon us."

Slowly, tentatively, Julia pulled down the covers so that she could see the Spirit standing before her.

He was even shorter in person than she had guessed, standing no taller than a twelve-year-old boy. And though it was nearly dark in her room, the apparition appeared to glow, emanating with a subdued yet spectacular white light.

"Who are you?" she croaked, amazed though still terrified of the specter in front of her.

"I am the Ghost of Christmas Past. Your past," was the seemingly harmless reply.

Finding herself at a loss for words, Julia heard herself asking the one question she desperately wished not to know the answer to, "Why are you here?"

"Your redemption," came the most unwelcome response, though Julia didn't dare call it a *humbug*.

"Come and take my hand," said the Spirit impatiently. "We have much to see and the hour is short."

With great trepidation, Julia cautiously crawled out of bed and put on her robe. Then, with only a moment's more hesitation, she grabbed the Spirit's extended hand.

They passed through the window and Julia saw the town quickly vanish below them. Suddenly it began to snow furiously as a humble, rural village slowly came into view. Julia gasped as she recognized the familiar landmarks of her childhood —the solitary country church, the rustic two-room schoolhouse, and the town's sole gas station/ supermarket/diner.

Her eyes began to moisten as memories from her youth flooded back upon her. There was the hill where they would go sledding, and the park by the creek where she had her first kiss. And in the distance lay the vast corn fields where she detasseled in the summer heat.

As they passed by the church, the sight of the cemetery caused Julia to pause momentarily. Her mother had been buried there, though she noticed the location was barren and unmarked. This vision, Julia realized with trembling expectation, must be of those happy early years before the shadow of that fatal diagnosis.

The Spirit gently prompted her and soon they stood before a modest dwelling on the outskirts of town that she had once called home. The squat, single story ranch house was plain but kept with care. A single strand of Christmas lights was strung from the roof, scarcely illuminating the lone snowman as he stood sentry in the dark.

They could hear laughter and singing coming from the house, and the wafting smell of roast pork caused Julia's stomach to growl with hunger. Parked by the curb were nearly half a dozen cars wrapped snuggly under blankets of heavy white snow. On the front porch were scattered numerous sleds, discarded remnants of the day's earlier adventures.

They passed through the front door and found themselves in the midst of euphoric Yuletide cheer.

Women were laughing and preparing the table, while the men talked about the weather and kept an eye on the playing children. In the corner sat a very pregnant woman with her young daughter waiting on her every need.

"Mother!" Julia cried at the sight of her and her mother.

"They cannot see you nor hear you," the Spirit cautioned. "They are but shadows of the past and nothing more."

Julia slowly approached the woman, tears streaming down her face. This was a sacred memory of innocence and joy, born before her acquaintance with pain. It was her favorite Christmas, the last one when everything seemed right with the world.

True, her parents were both unemployed at the time. But she had hardly noticed for the hardship was mitigated by unemployment benefits and food stamps. Nor was there any concern for the pregnancy once they enrolled in Medicaid. For Julia, the only difference between this Christmas and all the others before it was that her parents were home more often.

Much to Julia's distress, the scene abruptly changed and she and the Spirit were standing in the dinning room of another house.

"Why did you do that?" Julia angrily asked as her childhood innocence once more receded into the distant past.

"Just watch," came the simple command.

Julia looked and saw a family of four sitting at the table for Christmas dinner, each feasting on a single serving of meatloaf. Beside the two children sat their presents—a toy soldier for the boy and a doll for the girl.

"Is that Becky?" Julia asked, recognizing the girl as a classmate from school.

"Yes," the Spirit confirmed. "This is how she spent her Christmas while you cared for your pregnant mother."

Julia noticed that Becky's mother was also quite pregnant, though she didn't remember that Becky had any younger siblings. While the family appeared happy, the mood was subdued with just a hint of melancholy. The house was lightless but for the dining room, and the air felt chill with the thermostat turned down to a meager 60 degrees.

There was a small, pitiful tree adorning the living room, an unwanted sapling borrowed from the closed tree lot earlier in the day. It was shrouded in shadow as if ashamed of its appearance, standing bereft of lights or even a star upon its crown. Its sole apparel were a few homemade ornaments and a chain made of red-and-green paper.

When dinner was finished and the table cleared, the father donned his coat and, hugging his family goodbye, left into the cold, dark, winter night.

"Where is he going?" asked Julia, puzzled by this strange holiday behavior.

"To work."

"To work? But it's Christmas?" came the startled response.

"Yes, but he works the night shift at the spring factory the next town over. Tomorrow is already tonight for him," the Spirit replied.

"Factory?" Julia asked incredulously. "I thought he owned the body shop in town."

"He does. But his wife was just laid off and they need the money. He works nights at the factory and runs the body shop during the day, catching a few hours of sleep each evening."

Outraged, Julia demanded to know why someone would be so heartless as to fire a pregnant woman.

"Because," the Spirit gently explained, "her employer could no longer afford the payroll taxes. Her take home pay wasn't a problem, but it was the tens of thousands of dollars the employer had to pay into unemployment insurance, Medicaid, and other government charities that were bankrupting him. He had to lay off twelve employees this month just to stay in business and employ the remaining thirty."

Julia stood there speechless, defiant and offended. Was the Spirit really implying that Becky's family was suffering so that her's did not? That her family was supported by the labor and pain of those subsequently made worse off? But, her family needed these government services.

Besides, why didn't Becky's family enroll in these programs? If they suffered, it was because of their own fault.

"They don't qualify," said the Spirit in response to her unspoken question. "Even if they were willing to trade self-respect for money involuntarily taken from someone else, the government has determined that they aren't poor enough for such 'charity.' They must either work or they will not eat."

There it was again, the outrageous implication that her family was eating for free off the exhausting labor of others. An image, most unwelcome, came suddenly to mind as she saw her family on a plantation, living off the slavery of those working their fields. But, Julia consoled herself, they needed the help.

"Did you ask for help?" the Spirit's pointed question intruded upon her attempt at self-justification. She knew they did not. None of their friends in town were aware of their plight, and her parents had specifically instructed her not to tell their Christmas guests. She knew that help would have been forthcoming, if only they'd asked.

But her parents would rather quietly, anonymously fleece their neighbors than honestly admit they needed help. With a pang of guilt, Julia recalled Marlee's words from earlier that evening: "These are the people that I have harmed in life. The people that I have stolen from and wronged. In life I suspected they existed, though I refused to see the pain I was causing."

Chagrined at her callous indifference, Julia turned a mournful gaze upon the mother as she rested with her feet up.

"What," she asked with growing fear, "happened to the baby since she doesn't qualify for Medicaid?"

"He was stillborn," the Spirit informed her somberly, "buried only a few feet from where your mother now rests. Shortly thereafter the parents filed for bankruptcy, unable to repay the crushing medical bills. Would you like to visit the other eleven laid off workers?"

At that Julia broke down in tears. "Please," she begged the Spirit, "no more. Show me no more visions."

"We still have much to see," the Spirit said as he gave a wave of his hand. Soon the scene changed and she saw herself singing a solo in the church Christmas program. She had coveted the part, desiring the opportunity to show off the vocal skills that she had dreamed would one day make her a star.

But then the news came a week before Christmas that her mom had cancer. The prognosis was hopeful, but only if she received the medical treatment she needed. Thankfully, she had recently begun working as a secretary in a steel company and would soon be eligible to participate in their health insurance program. The carrier didn't want to cover her, but recently-passed legislation now prohibited insurance companies from refusing those with preexisting conditions.

So while this Christmas was tinged with fear, Julia's family was cautiously optimistic that the cancer would soon be in remission with the proper medical care. Now Julia no longer sang her solo entirely for her own vanity, but also for her mother sitting in the front row. The only thing she wanted that Christmas was for her mother to live so that she could see Julia become a famous singer.

Julia sighed ruefully at the memory. Pleasant in its wishfulness, it was a painful reminder that no one was in complete control of their own destiny. As much as Julia had spent her life pretending otherwise, she was not omnipotent and therefore not worthy of self-absorption, much less worship.

The sounds of the congregation enthusiastically applauding her performance suddenly brought Julia out of her reverie. As she focused once more on the vision before her, she remembered how loving and supporting the church had been throughout her mother's battle with cancer. They cooked meals for them, babysat Julia and her younger sister while her parents were at the hospital, and even helped out with repairs and chores around the house.

With a sense of irritation, however, Julia saw Fred and Teresa, their next-door neighbors, sitting next to her parents. Fred and Teresa were especially kind to them during this time, almost becoming a second set of parents to Julia and her sister. They took them to soccer practice and voice lessons and helped them with their homework.

They would give her parents money, even loaning them a car when her dad's truck broke down. Fred would mow their lawn and shovel the walks, while countless nights Teresa stayed up crying and praying with Julia's mother. They were a blessing that greatly eased her family's suffering during this time.

But then tragedy struck as Fred was diagnosed with leukemia, and Julia resented him for it. She knew she shouldn't, but she couldn't help it. She was jealous of him. Not because she wanted leukemia, she didn't; but she was envious of the love and support the church poured out on him. Her family was still well cared for by the congregation, but the church body had sacrificed so much of their time and money to help Fred and Teresa.

Julia grudgingly admitted to herself that such sacrifice was not out of favoritism towards Fred, but because his family's needs were greater than hers. Her mother was getting the medical care required, and every need they had was joyfully met by the congregation.

Fred, on the other hand, was not getting the medical care that he needed because he didn't have health insurance. His insurance had lapsed just weeks before he was diagnosed with leukemia, and his family made too much money to qualify for Medicaid.

So the congregation sacrificed to raise money so that Fred could get the treatment he needed. They established a benevolence fund, held special offerings, put on bake sales, raffles, and other fundraisers, and managed to raise $100,000 for Fred's medical expenses. A doctor in the congregation even agreed to prescribe the needed medication at no cost to Fred.

And so Julia was jealous of all the attention Fred received and resented him for it. But above all, she hated the fact that there was such suffering in the world because of the lack of universal health care. At least her mother received the care she needed, no thanks to the insurance company. If it were up to them, they would've let her mother die without a second thought. Thank goodness the government forced them to have some resemblance of a conscience.

"Do you know why his insurance lapsed?" the Spirit interrupted her silent rant.

Julia slowly shook her head in the negative as a sense of foreboding overcame her. She was suddenly quite certain that she did not want to know the answer, afraid that she had just been heaping resentment upon yet another link in her chain.

"He could no longer afford his premiums," came the simple response.

Julia sighed with relief. That was it? That wasn't her family's fault, but his own for not doing a better job budgeting. And to think that the church sacrificed so much for him when he was unwilling to sacrifice so little to keep his health insurance.

"His premiums skyrocketed after insurance carriers were no longer allowed to discriminate against those with preexisting conditions," the Spirit explained. "He could either pay the increased premiums or the mortgage, but not both. He was relatively young and in good health, so he opted to put a roof over his family's head rather than pay for insurance he didn't think he would need for awhile."

There it was, the insinuation that Fred did not have health insurance so that her mother could. But why, she wondered, did the premiums have to skyrocket?

"Because it isn't cheap to cover preexisting conditions," the Spirit answered. "This is why they weren't covered in the first place. It wasn't because insurance carriers had no soul, but because their customers couldn't afford it."

Julia suddenly remembered an illustration that opponents of the legislation had used. They had argued that forcing insurance companies to take those with preexisting conditions was like making home insurers cover houses that were already engulfed in flames. Unable to refuse to cover such exorbitant costs, the companies would have to find the money by requiring their current customers to pay more.

"Fred was hardly the only one to suffer, for tens of thousands of other families also went without insurance because they could no longer afford it," the Spirit continued, compounding Julia's guilt many times over.

She could feel her cheeks dampen with tears and her lips tremble in grief, unable to comprehend the extent of the suffering by thousands so that her mother could have insurance. Who was she to force so many to choose between health insurance and paying the mortgage just so her mother could get medical care? She loved her mother fiercely, but what made her so special that so many had to suffer for her benefit?

This, Julia reminded herself, was why government needed to provide universal healthcare for everyone. Then everyone would be covered regardless of income or preexisting conditions.

"Julia," the Spirit gently said, "someone else is always going to have to pay for preexisting conditions. Universal healthcare simply shifts that cost from the insured to the taxpayers. Fred and the others may receive health insurance but, after paying taxes, they may not be able to afford their homes, or their car notes, or their groceries."

"But," Julia protested, "surely there must be some government solution to this health care crises. Would you simply let all these people suffer?"

"Did the government provide you with car insurance?" the Spirit said, seemingly changing topics.

"No," Julia looked confused.

"When did you get it?"

"When I got my first car."

"And you were free to pick from a myriad of different plans and choose the right one for you at the price you wanted?"

"Yes," Julia grudgingly admitted. She didn't like where she saw this was going.

"And are any taxpayers being forced to subsidize your car insurance?"

"No," was the sullen response.

"That is the free market at work," the Spirit explained. "If the health insurance industry similarly operated in a free market, a person could buy the health insurance plan they wanted as soon as they turned eighteen and keep it for the rest of their lives. They could even buy reinsurance plans that would cover any rate increases should they develop cancer or leukemia. And all of it is done voluntarily, without the government forcing some to pay for others."

Julia didn't like the free market. Too much risk. Too much personal responsibility. Too few government bureaucrats telling her what to do. But she had to admit that the Spirit had a point. If it worked for car insurance, why couldn't it work for health insurance? And who gave government the power to decide who must pay for someone else's medical care?

She did, she reluctantly acknowledged. She and a majority of her fellow voters had deigned to make some the slaves of others. It was all done in the name of compassion, of course, but that compassion always came at someone else's expense. Julia shuddered with repulsion as she perceived just how profoundly evil and dehumanizing a government was that sacrificed some for the sake of others. It was no better than the slavocracy of the antebellum South.

As Julia was still trying to process this, the scene suddenly changed and she and the Spirit found themselves in the hallway of an apartment complex. The landlord, accompanied by a police officer, was loudly knocking on a door with a bright pink eviction notice taped to it.

A very tired, haggard man finally answered on the seventh knock, his eyes red from a combination of tears and alcohol. His wife was busy packing the rest of their meager possessions while unsuccessfully attempting to hush their crying children. A half empty bottle of vodka sat on the kitchen counter, haphazardly surrounded by a half-dozen empty "trophies" of recent vintage.

The landlord told them it was time to go, and the officer offered to give them a hand with their belongings. The father begged for more time, imploring for mercy on Christmas Day. The landlord, however, refused to relent, explaining that the new tenants were moving in the next day.

With hopeless resignation and heavy hearts, the man and his family packed their few earthly treasures into their car. With no place to store them and no way to transport them, the family had no choice but to leave behind their furniture. Finally, despite the loud protestations of his children, the man gave their dog to the landlord for they had no way to care for it.

After taking one last swig of vodka and giving the rest to the officer in thanks for his assistance, the man got behind the wheel and drove off with his family to destinations unbeknownst even to them. The only reminder of the season was the eighteen-inch miniature Christmas tree that stuck out of a box in the back seat, resting rather miserably between the two distraught, comfortless children.

Hesitantly, Julia turned to the Spirit as the landlord began the thankless task of readying the apartment for new tenants while his family celebrated Christmas without him. Though perplexed at the heart-wrenching scene she just witnessed, Julia was terrified at the explanation he might give.

"What was your mother's last job?" the Spirit inquired.

"Secretary for a steel company," she replied as she tried to guess what her mother's job had to do with the poor family now made homeless on Christmas.

"The man was the third-shift foreman at a factory that made motorhomes. He was laid off several months ago after the new steel tariff was passed."

Julia stood there confused, inferring that the tariff cost this man his job but not understanding how. After all, weren't tariffs a good thing? Didn't they help to protect American companies and American workers from competition overseas? For without them, her parents had told her, her mother might have lost her job.

"Tariffs," the Spirit continued, "are only able to protect certain domestic industries by making the products of their foreign competition more expensive." In this case, the Spirit explained, cheap foreign steel had flooded the country, which was great for those who bought steel but bad for domestic companies that produced it. Instead of competing by lowering prices, domestic steel companies such as her mother's had lobbied for the tariff to make the foreign-produced steel more expensive.

While they could now compete without having to become efficient and cost-effective, it also meant severe cutbacks for all those companies who had thrived by buying cheaper steel. Now with more money going to the purchase of steel, they had less money available for other supplies, renovations, research and development, marketing, and employees.

"In an effort to make a profit despite the artificially inflated steel prices," the Spirit concluded, "the motorhome company eliminated the third-shift as part of its cost-cutting efforts. Fifty employees were let go at his plant alone. Nationwide, the trickle-down effect of the tariff cost tens of thousands their jobs."

Julia was stunned at the enormous suffering caused by such a seemingly simple and benign government action. The government had decided to save the job of her mother and others in the steel industry at the expense of this man and thousands like him. By what guiding principle did the government pick such winners and losers, she wondered, other than who had the most political clout?

There certainly wasn't any moral standard that she could deduce that made one job more valuable than another. In fact, Julia was beginning to find the idea of the government picking winners and losers morally repugnant. It was a denial of the equal protection of the law; not because of race or gender, but because of political cronyism. While she was thankful for her mother's job, it sickened her that it was saved at the expense of someone else's simply because the steel industry and their unions had more political muscle.

With a slight smile on his face as he saw the makings of a wondrous transformation in Julia's character, the Spirit gave a small wave of his hand and they were once more in her childhood home. She recognized it as her last Christmas before she graduated from high school and went off to college.

Her younger self sat at the table with her father and younger sister, joined this year by only their neighbors Fred and Teresa. Julia's eyes moistened with tears as she saw her mother's empty seat opposite her father's. Her father had once made the mistake of sitting in that sacred place, but after a tantrum by Julia had promised never to do so again.

Julia was ashamed as she saw the obvious disdain and resentment with which her younger self treated Fred. Despite the odds and lack of health insurance, her neighbor had, with no small help from the community, survived his bout with leukemia and appeared as healthy as he ever had. And Julia had hated him for it, wishing, though she knew she shouldn't, that he had died in place of her mother.

The talk that Christmas was the news that Julia had just been accepted into the computer engineering program at the Massachusetts Institute of Technology. In the throes of pride, Julia temporarily tolerated Fred's existence long enough to gloat at being the only person from her state admitted to MIT. She bragged about graduating with a job at Microsoft or Apple, or maybe starting her own company someday.

Julia cringed with embarrassment at she saw younger self filled with such self-idolatry. There is nothing wrong with self-confidence or pride in achievement, but what Julia had was an all-consuming desire for her own glorification that left no room for humility or genuine love. She got what she desired, and used whatever and whoever necessary to achieve her goals.

Lost in her self-reproach, Julia was startled to notice that the scene had changed and they were now standing in the dinning room of a quaint Victorian house. She recognized the old residence as the home of Brad, the valedictorian of her high school class. His parents had bought it the year he was born, and had spent the next eighteen years restoring it to its former glory. It was the only house in her town, or county, for that matter, listed in the National Registry of Historical Places.

Brad was brilliant. Everyone in town knew that. He had the highest GPA in school history, and that year's highest SAT score in the state. He had been building computers since he was out of diapers and, like her, dreamed of being the next pioneer in computer technology. They had a fiercely competitive relationship, each seeking to outdo the other in tests and science fairs. She had lost every time but, strangely, rather than resent him for it, she respected him for his ability.

Now, as she watched, he hardly touched the Christmas feast before him. He sat there with depression etched in his features, saying nothing as he stared blankly at his nearly empty plate. Occasionally he would stab at a pea, munch on his salad, or take a bite of roast duck. But eventually he gave up and pushed his plate away, resting his head in his hands.

His mother tried to comfort him, but he was inconsolable and shied away from her touch. Shrugging in resignation, his family finally left him in peace as they quietly cleared the table with silent pity in their eyes. For seemingly the one hundredth time, Brad pulled a folded letter out of his pocket and stared at it in futile hope that it would read the opposite of what it did.

Without asking, Julia knew what it must be. Her letter from MIT was printed on identical stationary, only its words contained a more joyous message. She knew that he was going to apply to MIT as well, but assumed that he had decided not to when she learned that she was the only one in her state that was admitted.

Puzzled, Julia wondered why she had been accepted while Brad had been rejected. He was smarter than her in every respect, and was a far better friend and leader in school. He even found time to start his own computer company, play quarterback for the high school football team, and volunteer at the local soup kitchen. He was everything a college would want in an incoming freshman.

"Except that he's a white, middle-class male," the Spirit interjected. "Forgetting Dr. King's dream that his children would be judged by the content of their character rather than the color of their skin, colleges now actively engaged in reverse racial discrimination. Those who never engaged in discrimination are now discriminated against to compensate those who had never been discriminated against."

The Spirit's words pierced her conscience as tears once again welled up in her eyes. Knowing that MIT had an affirmative action program, Julia had gone to great lengths to stress her Cherokee Indian heritage. She had even thought about sending in a picture of herself in traditional dress standing in front of a tepee, but common sense eventually overruled her desire to play up her victimhood.

The fact that she hadn't actually been a victim didn't deter her from playing the race card. In truth, it was impossible for her to be discriminated against because of her race when no one knew about it. Even she wasn't sure if she was actually of Cherokee descent.

Family legend had it that she was 1/32 Cherokee on her mother's side, but no one could state that with any degree of certainty. They did have high check bones like some Cherokee do, and they had Native American family recipes they used. But in her heart, Julia knew that high check bones and family tradition did not entitle her to special treatment at someone else's expense.

And even if it was true that she was Cherokee and had been discriminated against because of it, what right did she have to demand that Brad be punished for it? He had never discriminated against her or anyone else on account of race or gender, so why should he be denied a seat that he was more qualified for? How was it justice that her collegiate dreams were realized while his were dashed?

"What happened to him," Julia asked in growing trepidation.

"He did okay for himself. He managed to build his company into a profitable enterprise, but he was never afforded the opportunities and expertise that you were given. Though his company has now expanded to five employees, his business success has always been handicapped by his lack of a prestigious diploma. Your salary your first year out of college was larger than any he has ever had. He —"

"Stop it!" Julia interrupted, unwilling to hear any more. She was unused to these strange feelings of remorse, guilt, and self-loathing that beat on her heart one unstoppable wave after another.

Overwhelmed with grief, she wasn't sure if she could stand seeing any more living visions of the links of her chain.

"We are nearly done," the Spirit patiently replied, "but there is one more vision for you to see."

The scene transformed once again, and Julia was immediately greeted by the rich, magnificent notes of a violin playing a piece by Bach that she recognized but couldn't name. Before her eyes could adjust to the scene, Julia assumed that they were in a grand concert hall as a prestigious concert violinist performed a Christmas program.

She was startled, instead, to find herself in the living room of a small but cozy apartment. Before her stood a child not yet nine years of age, masterfully playing the violin as few living possibly could. He was surrounded by his mother and three sisters, all with their eyes closed as they sat enraptured by the music.

But then Julia noticed that they were crying. All of them. Giant, silent tears steadily made their way down the checks of both the violinist and his audience as the music continued unabated. She saw no apparent reason for their sorrow, but felt certain that soon she would learn that she was the source of it.

The music briefly ended, but quickly started up again as Julia recognized a concerto by Mozart. As the concert continued, Julia had the sense that she was watching a requiem; a final farewell to...to what? The boy? The music? The passing of a loved one?

"A farewell to beauty," the Spirit said. "This will be the final performance of the young man's life."

"What is going to happen to him?" Julia asked, wondering how she could possibly be responsible for his death.

"Do not worry," the Spirit consoled. "He will live to be an old man. But today he will lose a voice fit for the halls of heaven itself."

Julia now understood that the family did not mourn the pending demise of the child, but of his music. A boy with the talent to amaze the crowds at Carnegie Hall was inexplicably playing for the final time in his family's tiny apartment. With training and experience he could easily become the greatest violinist of his generation, but now Julia had the terrible sensation that she had robbed the world of such a treasure.

"How did you pay for college," the Spirit asked.

Though a seemingly innocuous question, Julia immediately understood the implication. Her father, now a single parent, could no longer afford to send her to college, so she qualified for several government grant programs for low-income families. Unlike student loans which had to be paid back with interest, she didn't have to repay the grants which covered four-years of tuition plus room and board at one of the most prestigious, and most expensive, universities in the world.

In the end, her six-figure college diploma was completely paid for by taxpayers. Again, Julia recalled Marlee's words from earlier that evening: "These are the people that I have harmed in life. The people that I have stolen from and wronged. In life I suspected they existed, though I refused to see the pain I was causing."

And now she was face-to-face with the mother who was forced to pay for Julia's college education at the cost of her own son's obvious talent. Because of tax increases to finance ever increasing college grant programs, the Spirit explained that the mother was no longer able to afford violin lessons for her son, or even pay for a full-size violin as he had outgrown his child's version.

Rather than prolong the inevitable, the child had decided to make this Christmas performance his last. He would sell the instrument back to the music store the next day in hopes that some other child could derive as much pleasure from it as he did.

The image of her family on a plantation living off the forced labor of others once more rudely intruded upon Julia's conscience. She had been able to skeptically dismiss the idea earlier, but now she understood in guilt-ridden horror the reality of the picture. She had, without any plausible moral justification, enriched herself by sticking her hand into other people's pockets.

Broken in spirit, Julia turned to the Spirit to beg him to leave her alone.   But he wasn't there. Suddenly afraid and alone, Julia frantically looked in all directions for any sign of him. But he was no longer there, and neither, she realized, were the boy and his family.

She was, once more, sitting by herself on her own bed in her own house.   Relieved and exhausted, too tired to think, Julia crawled into bed and was soon fast asleep.

It was five minutes after midnight.

STAVE THREE.

THE GHOST OF CHRISTMAS PRESENT

Dong! Julia woke with a start. The bells were welcoming in a new hour. But then silence. There was only one chime, signaling one o'clock. The hour appointed for her meeting with the second of three spirits.

But no one came. Sitting up, Julia's spirits sank as she saw that she was alone in her empty room. Part of her wished the night was over and her redemption complete. But if there was to be a second spirit, she would have preferred to meet it upon awakening rather than wait in fearful anticipation of its arrival.

Putting on her robe, Julia briefly flirted with the idea of pulling the fireplace poker out of the wall in the event she needed a weapon. But upon reflection, she realized that she no longer feared the supernatural specters themselves, but rather the visions they showed her. While the spirits would not harm her, she found the links of her chain to be painfully haunting.

Redemption, after all, is the arduous journey of repentance. The first step is the hardest—the agonizing acknowledgment that one has sinned. It is followed by sorrowful remorse for one's actions and the sincere vow to refrain from such behavior in the future. The final step is the recognition of the need to seek forgiveness and the desire to right the wrongs of the past.

Julia couldn't remember the last time she had taken such a journey, and she wasn't too eager to take this one now. Though she was slowly beginning to admit her need for repentance, she had no desire to see any more living visions of her victims. The guilt was too unbearable; the shame overwhelming. Ultimately, however, Julia realized that the only way she could rid herself of the links of her chain was to acknowledge and repent of them.

Only then would she have peace. Many seek to find peace either by pretending they have nothing to repent of or by ignoring the relentless call of their conscience with fleeting distractions. But such peace is only a temporary delusion that lasts until the facade is eventually broken. In contrast, genuine peace only comes through soul-cleansing redemption. The only viable cure to her guilt, Julia concluded, is by repentance rather than flight.

Having now persuaded herself to see her night of redemption through to the end, Julia walked to the window in earnest hope that she would see another midnight visitor making his way to her front door. Disappointed in seeing no one on the street below her, Julia resolved to search her house for any sign of the promised specter.

Her reconnaissance, however, was paused mid-stride as she noticed a glow around the edges of her bedroom door as if the light was on in the hall beyond. Strange, she thought, that she hadn't noticed that before. She was sure that she had turned off the light before secluding herself in the master bedroom.

As she stood there puzzling over the source of the light, she felt more than heard a gentle rumble of laughter climb the steps from the floor below her. A strange, bellowing voice reminiscent of thunder called her by name and bid her to join it.

Wary that the intruder may be natural rather than unnatural, she cautiously exchanged the sanctuary of her bedroom for the unknown perils lurking beyond. With a growing sense of alarm, Julia noticed that the light switch remained in the off position; the glow coming not from the ceiling fixture but from the stairwell leading to the main floor.

Tip-toeing to the head of the stairs, she peered around the corner and saw neither friend nor foe waiting at the bottom. With each step she descended the air grew warmer as the light increased in both intensity and heat. In disquieting disbelief, she felt wave after wave of notes crest upon her before she finally heard the sound of Christmas carols being quietly hummed by a mighty voice.

Turning the corner on reaching the bottom, Julia stood dumbfounded at the metamorphoses she saw before her. It was still her house, but the combined living/dinning room had been transformed into a great hall encased in a cove of living greens. Every form of holly, mistletoe, and ivy climbed the walls and hung from the ceiling, speckled abundantly with glistening berries shinning brightly in the glaze of the light.

Her dinning room table was sagging under its burden, filled to overflowing with every kind of holiday delight. Mounds of duck, pork, turkey, pheasant, deer, bear, salmon, bass, and catfish were piled high on the table, interspersed with casseroles, potatoes, fruits, vegetables, salads, and desserts beyond number.

Sitting enthroned at the head of this bountiful feast was a giant whose presence, even more than his size, dwarfed the room. His most noticeable characteristic was his contagious smile, followed closely by his infectious laugh that propelled listeners along its currents. He was a boisterous, merry spirit utterly enthralled with the joy of life, living each moment in a wondrous amazement.

He was clad in a pristine green robe that hung loosely on his mammoth frame. His crown of curly brown hair was adorned by a wreath of holly; his feet shod in leather sandals that, in the fashion of ancient Rome, rose to his knees. In his hand he held aloft a blazing torch, though the flame was barely noticed as the fireplace crackled and hissed with a giant roaring fire.

"Who are you?" Julia timidly inquired, intentionally avoiding looking him in the eyes. She could read no evil in their depths, but instead was afraid of the kindness and gentleness with which they gazed upon her. She wilted not out of a sense of danger but of shame, feeling unworthy of such empathy in light of the chain with which she had bound herself.

"I am the Ghost of Christmas Present," the Spirit thundered in joyous response, seeming to delight in the pronouncement of its name. No vanity marked this display, for Julia could perceive only an innocent, childlike elation in the giant's temperament.

"Please show me the links of my chain," she requested with a calm resolve that surprised her. "I am ready to renew my night of redemption."

"Take hold of my robe," commanded the Spirit as his countenance became slightly subdued at the task at hand.

As Julia did as she was told, her home was replaced by a snug little cottage on the edge of a lake that glistened in the sunrise. Julia cringed as she surveyed the cramped quarters of the single-story dwelling that contained only a combined kitchen/living room, bedroom, and bath.

Like the floor plan, the Christmas decorations were simple and utilitarian. A pre-decorated

Christmas tree stood in the corner of the great room, while on the front door a wreath welcomed visitors. Scattered throughout the house was a manager scene and a few holiday nick-nacks, the only other reminders of the Christmas season.

In puzzlement, Julia watched as an elderly couple appeared to be directing traffic as a family of seven emptied their moving trailer. Soon the great room was lined with moving boxes, suitcases, and sleeping bags as the invading horde quickly made it their home. The five children, all under the age of ten, set out to explore the pile of presents under the tree, while their exhausted and melancholy parents repeatedly thanked the elderly couple for their hospitality.

These are not mere holiday guests, Julia surmised, staring in bewilderment at the scene before her. How, she worried, were nine people going to share one bathroom? And what circumstances would drive the young family to make such an imposition on the elderly couple? Surely she couldn't be the cause of their apparent homelessness.

"What are you most famous for?" the Spirit asked as he turned his sympathetic gaze from the family to meet her eyes.

Understanding immediately what he meant, Julia turned away in shame from the compassion she saw in his glance. She knew his kindness was not just for the plight of the family before them, but for her as well. But how, she wondered, could someone love a person as despicable as she?

Despite her success, she was not famous for her website design company or for anything she had done with computers. Instead, she was famous for her activism on one issue above all others—contraceptives. "Reproductive rights" is how she had phrased it when, doing her post-graduate work at a Catholic university, she had demanded that their student healthcare plans include contraceptives.

She became the poster child for free birth control when the university refused to sacrifice their moral beliefs to pay for her consequence-free fornication. She didn't care about their religious scruples, convincing herself that her "right" to insurance-provided contraceptives trumped their right to religious liberty. She was never able to articulate how, exactly, except that it had something to do with women's rights and gender equality.

She had been flattered to testify before Congress on the issue, and had proudly stood behind the president as he signed an executive order mandating that businesses and organizations include contraceptive coverage on their health insurance plans. The president had given a moving speech at the signing ceremony, saying they were doing this to protect the rights of women like her. The president even gave her one of the signing pens, which she still has framed on the wall of her office.

The university, of course, sued to block the mandate, but before the courts could rule on it, a new president had been elected and reversed the executive order. It wasn't until two years ago that Congress finally enacted the mandate as the Julia Contraceptive Protection Act. She once again stood behind the president as he signed the new legislation, and another signing pen now hung on her office wall.

It was one of the proudest moments of her life; her immortality now permanently enshrined in the United States Code. Lawsuits challenging the bill had been filed even before the ink was dry, but the Supreme Court had recently upheld the legislation after a lengthy legal battle. Julia had been overjoyed at the news, relieved that the "bigots" were no longer able to hide behind their religion.

The Catholic businesses and charities who had brought the lawsuits, however, felt differently, Faced with violating their conscience or the imposition of crippling fines, many had no choice but to close their doors. Hundreds of thousands of people lost their jobs, but Julia hadn't cared. She didn't consider any price too high for the protection of women's "reproductive rights."

Until now. Face-to-face with a family made jobless and homeless by Julia's Act, she understood the enormous cost imposed by her selfishness. It wasn't that she had been denied the opportunity to buy contraceptives. But she had wanted more than mere access. She had wanted someone else to pay for them, even if doing so was a violation of their faith.

The former was called theft, the later religious persecution. And she had been the foremost advocate for such evil. Such statism. Such collectivism. She had used the power of the state to sacrifice others in order to unjustly enrich herself. She was, she suddenly realized, no better than a socialist who sought to command and control the economy for egalitarian ends.

"Spirit," Julia asked at last, "who is he?"

To her surprise, the Spirit explained that the man didn't even work for a Catholic business. Instead, he had worked for a company that supplied one of the largest art and craft retail chains in the country. That chain, however, was owned by a Catholic family, and when they closed their doors, his factory was forced to cut their workforce in half due to the decreased demand. After months without employment, his family was no longer able to pay the mortgage and had no choice but to move in with his parents.

Overwhelmed at the enormous trickle-down effect of her greed, Julia fell to her knees in inconsolable grief. She was even worse than a socialist, she sadly concluded, for at least they were honest about what they were doing. She, on the other hand, had exercised the same governmental control of the economy while pretending that she was doing nothing of the kind. The ends were the same, it was only the means that were different. Instead of actually owning companies, the state simply told them what to do.

"Come," the Spirit said gently after a few moments, "we still have much to see."

As Julia once again took hold of the giant's green garment, she saw the cottage by the lake fade away as the buildings and landmarks of her town came once more into view. With growing discomfort as they walked the familiar streets of her small village, Julia developed the disconcerting feeling of a stranger in a foreign land.

Unlike her childhood home, this town held precious few memories for her, either good or bad. Though she was loath to acknowledge it, the reality was that she was a recluse who sought desperately to drown out her loneliness with workaholism. Other than those she worked with, she avoided knowing anyone else in town.

Even her neighbors were aliens to her, their faces indistinguishable to her from any she might see in a photo lineup. It wasn't that she didn't care for them, but that such personal relationships took too much effort and emotional investment. It was much easier for the government to care for them. After all, Julia considered it the only family that everyone belongs to.

Now as they passed neighborhoods full of strangers, she became terrified at the realization of how alone and unloved she actually was. Even the bureaucratic dispensers of government charity neither knew her nor cared about her. Their job was just another job, and people were just another number. Their mission was simply to give away other people's money in a loveless transaction governed by bureaucratic red tape.

In contrast, Julia perceived with chagrin, a person would be treated as an actual human being at any one of the many private charities she had so despised. These charities existed because they genuinely loved the person as an individual, not as an abstract problem waiting for an impersonal government solution.

Charity, she finally began to grasp, meant nothing to either the giver nor the receiver absent a voluntary, personal sacrifice. Time and resources by the former; humility and gratitude by the later.

Her thoughts were interrupted when they finally came to a stop before a modest split-level house in a middle-class neighborhood that was fast loosing its luster. Alarmed, Julia recognized the house as the one her secretary Mary lived in with her family. How was it possible, Julia wondered with a growing sense of foreboding, that Mary could be one of her victims?

She noted with surprise a "For Sale" sign out front. Odd, Julia thought, that Mary hadn't said anything about wanting to relocate. She wondered what had possessed them to sell so soon after they had just recently bought the house.

Impatiently, the Spirit nudged her toward the door, and reluctantly Julia complied. The house was beautifully trimmed for Christmas with well-used but faithful decorations now nearly a decade old. A giant artificial tree towered in the corner, simply yet elegantly adorned with red balls and white lights.

Garland hung on the stairwell and above the living room window, intertwined with red ribbon and graced with red bows. Electric candles stood lonely sentinel in each window, and a miniature nutcracker stood in solitary silence near the blazing fireplace. The mantel was adorned by an ancient manger scene of hand-carved wood, while from it hung five red stockings, each inscribed with the name of a family member.

But despite the beauty of the scene, Julia noticed only a few scatterings of presents under the tree and that the stockings hung limp and empty from their perch. And though the table was set with the family's finest china, Julia saw that no food had been laid out for dinner.

Suddenly a knock on the door interrupted Julia's inspection, and she saw a lone visitor bearing a spiral ham in one hand and a gift in the other. After being relived of his burdens and blessing their Christmas, the stranger departed and soon was replaced by yet another. This one, too, bore both a present and a dish, as did the dozen or so visitors who followed. Soon the base of the tree was buried with presents as the family sat down to their Christmas feast, complete with Jesus' birthday cake.

"Spirit," Julia finally asked, "who were these strangers who brought the presents and Christmas dinner?"

"Members of her church," came the simple explanation.

"Why?" Julia asked, though she feared learning the answer.

"Finances have been tight ever since her husband lost his job six months ago, and their church wanted to make sure they had a bountiful Christmas."

Julia broke down in tears as she finally understood how Mary was, in fact, one of the links of her chain. Julia had worked at the same company Mary's husband did until she left several years ago after claiming that she had been a victim of gender discrimination.

In her lawsuit, she alleged that the executive who hired her had intentionally set her starting salary lower than her male counterparts. The ordinary statute of limitations had lapsed years ago, and the executive had long since passed away and was therefore unable to defend himself.

But under the Lilly Ledbetter Act, Julia was able bring her claim because her current bimonthly paycheck was still $1.53 lower than that of her average male colleague. She couldn't prove that this disparity was due to any current discriminatory policies, but argued instead that it was partly a result of the alleged discrimination at the time of her hire.

After eighteen hours of deliberation, the jury decided in her favor and awarded the largest damages verdict in state history. Six months ago, upon losing its final appeal, the company laid off a quarter of its workforce in an effort to pay the millions it owed her in damages. Scores of innocent people had lost their jobs simply because of her unsupported allegations that, due to the lapse of time, the company no longer possessed the evidence to disprove.

First with interest and then with growing distress, Julia noticed that she had become the topic of the dinner conversation. Mary's three children were blaming her for the loss of their dad's job, urging their mother to find a more benevolent employer.

Their father said nothing, but he didn't have to. Julia now understood why he had suddenly stopped talking to her, even going so far as to cross to the other side of the street rather than share the same sidewalk with her.

"Please," Mary admonished her children, "Julia did not intend for your father to lose his job."

"Perhaps not," conceded her eldest, "but she had to know that people were going to suffer so the company could pay her dubious damages."

With a flush of contrition, Julia recalled Marlee's words from earlier that evening: "These are the people that I have harmed in life. The people that I have stolen from and wronged. In life I suspected they existed, though I refused to see the pain I was causing."

"Selfishness blinds many people, even you on occasion," Mary gently chided her son. "Julia sees only what she wants to see, but I believe there is hope for her yet. Someday, I pray, she may find redemption for the wrongs she has done to others."

Julia stood astonished at such undeserved kindness. She had just cost her secretary's husband his job and forced them to put their house on the market, and yet Mary still loved her. Overcome with shame, Julia turned to the Spirit and begged him to take her back home.

"Your night of redemption is not yet complete," he said tenderly. "Take my robe, for we still have much to see."

Tempted to argue with the Spirit but prudently deciding against it, Julia once again grabbed his robe and saw Mary and her family fade away as the scene transformed once again. She immediately found herself assaulted with a wave of sullenness even before she saw a family silently eating their Christmas dinner.

From all appearances, everything but their attitudes appeared normal. The Tudor-style house still smelled brand-new and glistened with the latest appliances. Several newer-modeled cars occupied the three-stall garage, and in back a winterized swimming pool faced a breath-taking view of the mountains. The house was decorated extensively for Christmas, with presents piled high under the tree and a feast laid out on the table.

But despite this apparent lack of financial want, an unhappiness hung in the air so palpable that Julia could almost touch it. The two young children in particular ate their dinner with noticeable sullenness, though their parents were doing their fair share of moping as well.

"What is wrong with with this family?" Julia asked the Spirit, perplexed as to what wrong they had suffered.

"They were planning on spending Christmas vacation on sun-soaked beaches," came the reply. "They were going to spend a few days at Disney World, then they were going on a week-long Caribbean cruise."

"And why did they have to cancel their plans?" she asked, still confused over her culpability in their ruined holiday.

"They helped you finance your recent business expansion," came the simple response.

Like her original startup loan, Julia had taken out a second business loan from the Small Business Administration to help her hire new employes and afford an aggressive marketing strategy. She was one of thousands of small businesses who were able to take advantage of a massive increase in the SBA's loan program.

She had known that the loans were being financed by a large tax increase, but she hadn't stopped to consider the pain it was causing working families. But now, as she stared at the people she had robbed, she felt no remorse. After all, she reasoned, what was a missed vacation compared to the new jobs she was creating?

"Julia," the Spirit interrupted her attempted justification, "did you apply for a private loan for your expansion?"

"Of course," she defensively replied, "numerous times." But she had been rejected by sixteen different banks because they had considered her business plan too risky. Unlike the stingy bankers, however, the SBA was all too eager to invest in her visionary strategy, and now her business was one of the region's most successful website designers.

"You are an exception, not the rule," the Spirit cautioned her. "Not every SBA loan is a success story like your's. Tell me, who is a better investor of money—a person seeking profit or a government bureaucrat? Somebody with their own money, or with someone else's?"

Julia's mood suddenly became as sour as that of the family in front of her. Though she didn't want to admit it, she instinctively knew that the free market was a far better investor than the bureaucracy would ever be.

The job of an investor was to make a profit by prudently financing productive, efficient businesses that produced innovative products at prices consumers demanded. The job of a government loan officer, however, was simply to give away taxpayer money to businesses the free market considered too unprofitable.

And by forcibly robbing taxpayers to finance the unprofitable, they have less money to exchange with companies they believe would give them the most return for their money. This family had planned their holiday vacation by looking for all the best travel deals at the prices they were willing to pay, but now those efficient, profitable companies were deprived of business so that a government clerk could write a check to their well-intended but clueless competitor.

"Would you like to visit the thousands of employees these companies had to lay off because of decreased demand after the tax increase?" the Spirit pointedly asked.

Ashamed at the compounded consequences of her greed, Julia slowly shook her head as tears once again fled down her checks. In contrast to the free market in which money is voluntarily exchanged for mutual profit, she had forcibly taken from others in the blind pursuit of her unrelenting avarice.

There is no amount of utilitarian ethics, Julia realized, which can justify the unjustifiable. Theft is still theft whether committed by an investment banker or a meth-riddled addict. It is no less criminal simply because the robber is convinced he can use someone else's money more profitably. She trembled in shame as once more the unwelcome image of living on a plantation supported by the slavery of others planted itself firmly in her consciousness.

The Spirit once more instructed her to take hold of his robe, and as she did so she found herself surrounded by the din of plates and clamoring of voices of a dining hall. As the scene came into focus, Julia noticed with a start that she wasn't in a restaurant as she had imagined, but instead was in the midst of a homeless shelter's cafeteria.

The line for those waiting for food stretched out the front door and around the block, while inside the room nearly brimmed with almost three hundred hungry souls feasting on their Christmas dinner. Many of them were single, unwashed, middle-aged men whose eyes had long-since grown dim with hopelessness as poverty became their lifestyle.

But among them, Julia noted with surprise, were a number of women of all ages. Those with children still sought to maintain some resemblance of cleanliness as hope had not yet given way to the paralyzing fear that shimmered just below the surface. In sad contrast, however, those without children were even filthier than the men, as long ago self-loathing had vanquished any sense of self-worth.

The room was spartanly adorned with seasonal centerpieces and strings of red and green lights blinking above the windows. A large Christmas tree stood in one corner, piled high with such boring but essential presents as shoes, underwear, and sweaters for the children. In bewilderment, she saw the bell ringer from earlier in the evening handing out the gifts to the children who formed a long line around him.

Julia saw herself standing before a table occupied by one of the few intact families she saw at the shelter. They immediately stood out from the crowd, for it was obvious from their dress and appearance that they had just recently become acquainted with poverty. Awkwardness and embarrassment at their circumstances, rather than hopelessness, marked their countenances.

"Who are they?" Julia asked as the three children quickly ate their dinner while casting wary glances at the strangers around them.

"Their parents lost their jobs a few months ago," the Spirit somberly reported, "and they were evicted from their apartment last week. Without relatives nearby, the family had no choice but to move into the shelter."

"Why didn't they get on government assistance?" Julia instinctively inquired before she could reconsider the wisdom of her question. She now understood that such money was forcibly taken from others, but surely those in need were justified in taking what was already stolen.

"Because possessing stolen property is just as criminal as stealing it in the first place," the Spirit explained. "The parents neither wanted to become a party to an immoral act nor become dependent on its repetition. They were unwilling to look their children in the eye and tell them not to steal while they simultaneously lived off of the purloined money of others."

The parents' stubborn display of principled integrity dumbfounded Julia, who ruefully had shown so little of either principles or integrity throughout her life. Not that she was a bad person, she tried to convince herself. But her sense of morality had always begun and ended with what was best for Julia. She loved her neighbor as herself, so long as it didn't interfere with her love of herself.

"Why did they lose their jobs?" Julia finally asked, frantic to find a distraction to the loud reproach of her conscience.

"The ice cream factory where they worked laid off a dozen employees after its taxes were increased," the Spirit replied.

Julia had almost forgotten about the increase in sales and corporate income taxes because they didn't affect her. She had been one of the foremost advocates for tax breaks for internet-related companies, arguing that the industry couldn't possibly survive without them. Besides, she had insisted, the tax breaks weren't handouts, but rather simply allowed people to keep more of their own money.

Now as she stared at the family in front of her, she reluctantly realized that she was only able to keep more of her own money if the government instead took a larger portion from others. Taxpayers, Julia belatedly perceived, had to pay artificially inflated rates so that a few government-favored businesses could be taxed less.

She could no longer deny that it was in fact a government handout, albeit one that eliminated the bureaucratic middleman. Instead of taxing the ice cream company in order to give the money to her business, the ice cream company was taxed more so that her tax burden was lowered. It was a distinction without a difference.

And, she admitted to herself, she was only able to get this government subsidy because of very effective lobbyists who warned legislators of all the jobs that would be lost without it. Sadly, this family and others like them were forgotten by lawmakers, overlooked because they had no one to warn about the jobs that would be lost with the tax breaks.

Julia began to break down in tears as she realized that the government had picked some jobs at the expense of others. It was unfortunate when people lost their jobs in the ordinary ebb and flow of voluntary decisions in the free market. It was tragic but natural. But it was unforgivable, she realized, when jobs were lost because the government predestined certain industries over others in the marketplace.

"Do you know what the tax rate would be if all tax breaks were eliminated?" the Spirit interrupted her tears. When Julia refused to hazard a guess, the Spirit informed her that the government could raise the same amount of revenue simply by cutting rates in half and eliminating all tax breaks. Julia only cried harder.

After they had lingered a little while longer, the Spirit gently commanded her to grab his robe once more. Doing so, Julia suddenly found herself standing in the great room of a custom-designed, hand-built log cabin nestled in the mountains. In a feat of stylistic design, the cabin was both cozy and large, rustic and modern, at the same time.

A giant fireplace roared with life beside her, while in front of her stood the largest indoor Christmas tree she had ever seen. Upon inspecting it further, Julia was astonished to see that the evergreen had never been touched by an axe. Instead, the architect had built the cabin around the place the tree had called home for hundreds of years.

Beyond the tree stood a wall of windows with a breathtaking view of the mountains that left Julia awestruck. For years she had pretended she was a nature lover, fighting for legislation to protect endangered species and prevent deforestation. But, having eyes only for herself, she had long ago stopped visiting nature or finding any joy in it. She didn't like to be reminded of a beauty outside herself, of a creation that revealed the handiwork of a Creator.

Amazed but intimidated by the sight before her, Julia turned and saw an extended family eating their Christmas dinner at a table too small for both the crowd and the feast. But as Julia took in the scene before her, she noticed that the family was outnumbered by mountains of moving boxes. Every room but the kitchen appeared to be packed, either having just come off the moving truck or about to be loaded on it.

"Are they moving in?" she asked hopefully, uncertain as to the misfortune in front of her but confident that she was somehow the cause of it.

"Out," came the Spirit's joyless response as he turned to look at her. "The grandparents wanted to spend one last Christmas with their family before they had to sell the dream home they lovingly built themselves."

Julia turned away from the Spirit's gaze, still haunted by the undeserved kindness she saw in them. She had made people jobless and drove them from their homes, and she did it all in the name of greed disguised as compassion. She was nothing more than a thief who used the government to take what she wanted, and yet there the Spirit stood with unmerited grace in his eyes.

"Tell me, please, how did I cause them such misery?" Julia boldly asked. She was still unable to look him the eyes, but she knew that her only chance at redemption was to take responsibility for her sins.

"They lost their home so you could keep yours," came the blunt reply.

With that Julia covered her face with her hands to hide her shame as she wept at the suffering she had caused. She had nearly defaulted on her mortgage earlier in the year as she had struggled to stay current on monthly payments for a house that was worth less than what she owed on it.

But, as she did in nearly every crises in her life, she and other homeowners had cried out to the government to rescue them. Julia, who obstinately refused to bend her knee in prayer to God, had no qualms about such humble supplication to government. In revulsion, she now realized that she wasn't an atheist after all. She had a god, and his name was the state.

And, as it always did, her self-made god had bailed her out of her misfortune by visiting it on someone else instead. The government took other people's money, the only money it ever has, and paid the difference between her mortgage and what her house was worth. It then paid her mortgage company an incentive to refinance her remaining balance to more affordable monthly payments.

And to finance her bailout, the government significantly raised taxes on property valued over a million dollars. Unable to pay such exorbitant taxes, these grandparents had no choice but to relocate to more modest accommodations. They had spent their lives saving and then building a home to eventually pass on to their children, but now such a legacy had to be forfeited to pay for her mortgage.

"Come," the Spirit said as the family finished dinner and began to pack up the kitchen, "we have one more vision to see."

Julia grabbed his robe once more and heard the sound of children laughing and playing in a swimming pool. As the scene became clearer, she saw that they were watching a dozen children playing water volleyball in an indoor pool. Their fathers played a pickup game of basketball on the court across the hall, while by the locker rooms a few of their mothers used the treadmills of an extensive home gym.

Soon an announcement came on the intercom that the food was almost ready, and, after a quick shower, nearly fifty people sat down for Christmas dinner. The dinning room was exquisitely decorated for Christmas with lights, garland, candles, centerpieces, and even holly hanging from the chandeliers. In a clash of decor, however, a "Happy Birthday" banner hung over an elderly woman sitting at the place of honor, surrounded by piles of birthday presents.

"Who is she?" Julia asked.

"The owner's mother. She turns eighty years old today, and her family wanted to celebrate it with her."

"And who is the owner?"

"He founded an eye glass factory in town," the Spirit explained. "He started it twenty years ago, and now employs seventy-five people."

Julia was puzzled, for the family certainly didn't look like any of the victims she had seen before. They appeared happy, healthy, and so far removed from any fear of financial want that she wondered how it was possible that she could've wronged them.

"You demanded that they pay more in taxes so that you wouldn't have to," the Spirit answered her unspoken question.

Though Julia now understood, she didn't feel any remorse for her advocacy of the recent tax increase on the wealthiest two-percent. It was only right, she had argued, that the rich be made to pay their fair share, whatever that meant.

Besides, Julia defended herself, what did this family need the money for? Grant it, they weren't billionaires with private jets and yachts, but they weren't hurting for money either. They probably could live quite comfortably even if their income was cut in half. No one needs all this stuff any—

Julia stopped as she realized what she was doing. Out of spiteful envy, she wanted to cut this family down to size on the ridiculous theory that if she couldn't have it, neither should they. Like the communists before her, she had deemed it her right to use government force to tell this family how much they could make and to seize the rest in taxation.

By what right, however, did she have to ask someone else to pay more in taxes than she did? How was that equal protection under the law? And how can a government that is supposed to protect property rights simultaneously punish a man for having too much wealth?

With horror, Julia finally understood that a "fair" and "compassionate" tax system was a wealth redistribution scheme by which the majority confiscated the property of the minority. "Fair share" simply meant whatever was necessary so the majority neither had to raise their own taxes nor reduce their government benefits. It was a system built on selfishness rather than justice.

"Do you know what he was going to do with the money before you took it?" the Spirit interrupted her thoughts.

Julia thought of lavish European vacations and golf trips to sunny resorts, but she merely shook her head in the negative.

"He was going to reinvest it in his business by adding a night shift in January. He even had tentative plans for a large addition to the plant in the next five years."

With a start, Julia tearfully realized that her greed had not only cost additional jobs at this eye glass factory, but also at plants and businesses throughout the country. Enormous sums of wealth, squandered on the altar of her ravenous greed, could have been used for so much good if only left in the hands of their rightful owners.

Overcome with grief, Julia turned to ask the Spirit to take her home only to discover that she was already back in her own bedroom. Alone.

Slowly, ominously, the bells began to chime.

STAVE FOUR.

THE GHOST OF CHRISTMAS FUTURE

Dong! *Dong*! Then silence. Two o'clock in the morning. The hour of her appointment with the last of the three Spirits.

While waiting with strained ear for the approach of her supernatural visitor, Julia noticed with growing alarm a black mist forming near the foot of her bed. As the foreboding haze grew in both size and density, she saw a black robed figure suddenly arise from its midst.

The hooded specter stood before her tall and stately, obscured in so much shadow that she could only discern his eyes as they glowed with the pale orange light of an autumn moon. His lower half remained concealed in the ghostly fog with which he ensconced himself, while in his wraithlike hand he held a scythe whose blade flickered with a white hot heat.

Nearly overcome in fear at the unnerving apparition in front of her, Julia was tempted to run for the fireplace poker still embedded in the wall where she had thrown it. But with a great effort of will she finally resisted such foolishness, reminding herself that none of the spirits were there to hurt her. They were there to aid her on her journey to redemption, and killing her would make a mockery of their efforts.

"Are you the Ghost of Christmas Future?" Julia asked, taking a few tentative steps towards the phantom.

Though she received no verbal response, the Spirit gave a slight nod of the head while simultaneously the words *I am* were pressed upon her consciousness. Julia shuddered at the telepathic communication, petrified as she realized her thoughts as well as movements were exposed to his unblinking, penetrating gaze while he remained shrouded in shadow and darkness.

"Spirit," Julia said after calming herself, "I am terrified of you, though I know you mean me no harm. Please show me the visions of my future, for I wish to be rid of the chain by which I have bound myself. I must face my guilt before I can repent of it."

The words *very well* were heard by her mind's ear as the Spirit struck the floor with the handle of his scythe, enveloping both of them in the cloud of black mist. When the darkness finally receded to gird the phantom's waist, Julia noticed with trepidation that they were at the corner of her block.

She knew that this hour would reveal visions of the future, but she found herself trembling with fear of seeing the future Julia. The painful lessons of the night had torn away the mask of her true nature, and she was loath to see the conclusion of the path she had chosen. It was distressing enough to see the victims of her greed, but the thought of seeing herself as a miserable old hermit nearly caused her to lose her resolve.

The Spirit pointed with a spectral hand toward her house, and reluctantly she fell in step beside him. She noticed that he moved silently, gracefully in the mist, almost as if he floated rather than walked in its midst. His stride, if it was a stride, was quick, and Julia found herself jogging just to keep up.

Just as they did earlier this evening, carolers were entertaining the house next to hers. But as they finished their performance, she observed with chagrin that they quietly, almost fearfully, tip-toed past her house in search of more receptive audiences. Approaching her home, Julia's face flushed with embarrassment as she saw the lawn littered with "No Carolers" and "Caroler Free Zone" signs, emphatically punctuated with a giant chain blocking entry to her front stoop.

Walking with the Spirit through the front door, she paused in the entryway as her eyes adjusted to the darkness that surrounded them. A single lamp glowed in a distant corner of the house, and the faint sound of a television came from somewhere in the basement. Julia began to wonder if her future self was even home, partly hoping that she might be secluded in self-imposed isolation in a distant, remote cabin.

She saw that the picture of herself and Marlee at their ribbon-cutting ceremony was still there, though as she looked at it in the moonlight it appeared that Marlee's face was contorted in silent, haunting weeping.   The other pictures, Julia anxiously noticed, were of a young boy.

Zachary.   The name planted itself firmly in her consciousness, and Julia knew that it must be the name of her son. She paused as she came upon a frame with Zachary's baby picture on one side and his adoption papers on the other. According to the certificate, she had adopted him twenty years ago as she was about to turn forty-one years of age.

He was a cute baby.   A little chubby, as most babies are, but quite adorable. He had wavy blond hair and mischievous blue eyes that both amused and concerned you.   As she studied the other pictures in the house, she noticed with apprehension that both the chubbiness and mischievousness remained as he grew older. Unlike the Julia she had been before tonight, she now found herself more disturbed by the later trait than the former.

The most recent photograph she saw of him was his high school graduation. Husky would have been a charitable description of him.   He stood slightly over six feet and weighed in at nearly 300 pounds.   Though he stared at the camera with a cocky grin as he received his diploma, Julia knew instinctively that he was an underachiever who was lucky to even graduate with his class.

His eyes were still mischievous, but now they appeared hardened with a cruel selfishness. Yes, she realized beyond a shadow of doubt, this was her son. Not biologically, of course, but he had inherited her identical spirit of nihilistic selfishness. Soon enough he, too, would be bound by a chain of his own making.

Her inspection was interrupted by a ghostly finger pointing up the stairs, and Julia obediently followed the phantom with legs weak with fear. Upon entering her bedroom, Julia gasped in humiliation as she saw her future self sprawled out on the bed in a drunken stupor.

Empty bottles of rum and whiskey were scattered throughout her room as destitute testaments of the joyless existence her life of greed had brought her. Julia recoiled in horror as she observed that her future self had spent her drinking spree stabbing out the eyes that had stared back at her from framed pictures of herself with Zachary. Apparently the guilt of what she had wrought was too much for her to bear.

Without surprise, Julia noted that the ring finger of her future self was bare without even the hint of a tan line. Nothing in the house had suggested that she had ever married or even had a boyfriend. She was the sole object of her heart's affections, and she doubted that a child was capable of occupying more than the tiniest corner of her world.

The Spirit pointed again, and this time she eagerly followed him away from the self-destruction before her. They followed the sound of the television to the basement, where all 350 pounds of Zachary sat surrounded by donuts and chips as he played video games in a mindless daze.

At first Julia was relieved to see that he wasn't using drugs, but then the panic returned tenfold as she saw on the screen the alternating scenes of cold-blooded murder and sadomasochism that vied with each other in their gruesomeness. Her son, having grown up under a roof in which God was dead, found life meaningless and morals inconvenient. His will, imposed by violence, was the only thing real to him. It was the lodestar—the only star—of his moral compass.

On the coffee table in front of him, Julia noticed a sizable disability check made out to him that he had yet to find time to cash. Other than self-absorbed laziness, Julia could observe no visible disability that hindered her son from gainful employment.

It isn't that he can't work, the Spirit's words imposed themselves on her mind, *it's that he won't*. Julia knew then that Zachary was defrauding taxpayers with a non-existent disability. It was immoral enough to be living off of other people's stolen money, but to do so under false pretenses was despicable.

It was your idea. You helped and encouraged him. The thought was like a slap against Julia's conscience. With a start, she realized that she was gazing at another link in her chain. Zachary, though responsible for his own decisions, was who he was in large part because of her. Sobbing uncontrollably, she understood that he was a future victim of her all-consuming, never-quenching narcissism.

This does not have to be, the Spirit's unheard words sought to comfort her. *These visions have not yet come to pass and may still be unwritten. He does not have to be a victim.*

"Spirit," Julia vowed between her tears, "I will not write this future. Please, take me from this place of perdition."

The scythe once again smote the floor, causing the black fog to encompass them in a darkness so profound that not a single ray of light could penetrated its shadows. Unable to see the Spirit or even her hand in front of her face, Julia felt an inescapable sense of intense loneliness compounded by overwhelming regret as images of her victims flashed in a constant slideshow before her conscience.

This is what hell must be like, she suddenly perceived, a place of eternal solitary confinement in which one's sole company were the haunting sins of one's past. No excuses. No self-justifications. No self-deceit. No alcohol-induced numbness. Just the torment of agonizing, never-ending guilt punctuated with ceaseless self-hatred for obstinately refusing to repent during life.

Just as quickly as it arose, the cloud receded once more to rest around the phantom's legs. But not before Julia's shirt became soaked with sweat from the vision of eternal damnation that awaited her. She was thirsty, so very thirsty, and found herself incapable of stilling her trembling hands. Overcome with emotion, she fell to her knees in humble gratitude that she had been given this night of redemption to avert such a future.

When she had finally calmed herself, Julia looked up and saw that they were in a modest brownstone rowhouse badly in need of repair. The front window was broken, replaced not with a new one but with a pane of two-by-fours that kept both villain and sunlight at bay. Stress fissures pockmarked the far wall, standing exposed as the faded wallpaper had begun to peel off in strips.

The staircase climbed at a slight decline from the wall to which it was attached, the slope unguarded by a railing which had long-since fallen away. The discolored carpet had been worn thin with constant foot traffic, while the thread-bare furniture lacked both comfort and style as it approached its third decade of existence.

An extended family gathered for Christmas dinner in a dining room marked more by the mold and watermarks on the ceiling than the feast on the table. At first Julia assumed that the house was filled with holiday guests, but as she looked more closely she noted a decided lack of sleeping bags and luggage.

Instead, as she counted three generations sitting around the table, she came to the realization that the grandparents, their two sons and a daughter-in-law, and four children all lived under the same roof. Why, she thought, would three families share a home built for one?

It's cheaper, the Spirit silently explained. *The divorced son lives in the basement with a son of his own. His older brother shares an upstairs bedroom with his wife and son, while their two daughters live in the other spare bedroom across the hall.*

Cringing at the cramped living arrangements, Julia wondered how she could have forced the sons to move back in with their parents, this time with families of their own. It was obviously cost-effective, but certainly they could have afforded their own homes.

Because of hyperinflation, few families can afford the luxury of their own homes, the Spirit continued. *Multi-generational housing has become the norm out of necessity, not out of choice. Only by pooling resources can they barely pay for such things as housing, a car or two, groceries, and utilities that they once took for granted.*

Julia stood there confused. Hyperinflation? She remembered reading that after World War I, hyperinflation among the defeated Central Powers caused the prices of goods in Germany to doubled every two days and inflation in Austria to grow nearly 1500%. Though the scene in front of her didn't look quite so dire, she was puzzled as to how rampant inflation could have begun in her own country.

The government wasn't able to tax enough to satisfy your greed for other people's money, so it had to borrow it. When it borrowed too much, investors stopped buying its treasury bonds. Instead, the government simply printed more money with which it bought its own debt. All this fiat money, however, exceeded demand, and within a few short years hyperinflation set in.

Julia wept in terror at the implications of the Spirit's words: all of her countrymen were among her future victims as her avarice contributed to nationwide hyperinflation. Inflation was a tax that no one, rich or poor, could escape. And it was a form of taxation that most current payers never voted for, having resulted from policies and decisions made a generation earlier.

The seeds of her selfishness, planted years ago, had now yielded a harvest of millions of victims. Her chain had become immeasurably long, made up of links too numerous to count. Sinking to the floor under its crushing weight upon her conscience, Julia begged the Spirit to take her back home.

When we are finished, the Spirit reproached her as his scythe once more struck the ground and engulfed them in his black mist. As the fog receded around her, Julia saw that they were standing in a brick colonial home that was decorated more with moving boxes than with Christmas decorations.

Dressed in his service uniform, an army major sat with his wife and four children as they opened their meager presents. Each child only received two gifts, a necessary clothing item and either a book or a toy. No video games. No electronic gadgets. Nothing that wasn't on clearance from the dollar store. The parents shared a single present— a plastic bulb ornament with a recent family photograph enclosed inside.

The artificial Christmas tree remained the only decoration yet to be packed. Most of the house was already stowed in boxes, divided into categories marked "charity," "trash," and "Fine, we'll take it with us." In consternation, Julia noticed that the later pile was considerably smaller than the first two.

The table was carefully set with red and green plastic place settings, awaiting the two store-bought pizzas that were lazily baking in the oven. The meal's only resemblance to a Christmas feast was the homemade birthday cake that adorned the center of the table. "Happy Birthday, Jesus!" was inscribed on its white chocolate surface, with a single red candle punctuating the message.

The banging of the flag pole hooks drew Julia's attention, and she saw that the flag still proudly hung in its place. As she glanced outside, however, she was surprised to see that the family resided on a military base. Or at least it used to be a military base.

A long line of moving vans stood lonely vigil before every house on base. Semi-trailers were parked in front of office buildings, ready to move files and furniture to their next destination. Most of the army vehicles, humvees, and other equipment were no longer on base, already relocated to their new homes.

"What is the meaning of this?" Julia demanded with patriotic furor as she turned to the phantom. "Why does this base have to close? Why are these families moving?"

So the government can provide you with retirement checks, the Spirit replied. *At first the major had to pay five percent more in taxes to pay your social security. Then he saw a ten-percent increase. Then a twenty-percent increase. Now he and most of those on base have lost their jobs to military cuts so the government can continue to send you checks.*

Julia stood there dumbfounded, unable to understand what the Spirit was telling her. She had paid into social security all her working life. That was her money, and she was entitled to it. Why would this major have to pay for her retirement with either higher taxes or his job?

The government no longer has your money. As soon as it cashed it, it turned around and gave it to your father. Each generation works to pay for the retirement of the one before it. When they can't be taxed anymore, the government is forced to cut defense spending to pay for welfare spending.

The Spirit's unheard words once again brought to her mind the unwelcome image of herself as a southern plantation owner living off of the slave labor of others. By what moral right did she have to force other people to pay for her retirement?

Sure, her future self may no longer be able to work. But were antebellum slaveowners any more justified in refusing to free their slaves because doing so would financially ruin them in their old age? Besides, she had had an entire lifetime of labor to prepare for her retirement.

And when saving and investing wasn't enough, children and grandchildren would voluntarily step in to provide a safety net. Her own grandfather had lived with them until his death the year before her mother's diagnoses with cancer. That is what families are for—to be a nucleus of love and support in an uncertain world full of unfairness.

Julia suddenly began to laugh at herself as she realized how foolish she was to have ever trusted the government with her retirement in the first place. Her face became flush with embarrassment at how gullible she had been when politicians had promised her that her money was being stored safely in a lock box somewhere.

Rule number one, Julia somberly concluded, was to never trust a politician. Rule number two, never take money from the government. That money is always someone else's to which the recipient invariably becomes addicted to. And that addiction comes with a price—slavish obedience to the hand which feeds it. A person can't really be a free citizen if he is dependent on the government for his basic substance.

Suddenly a thud interrupted Julia's introspection as the scythe hammered the floor and they were once again enveloped in a black cloud. As the mist retreated, Julia found herself in a small, frugally furnished one-bedroom apartment.

Everything she saw appeared magnified: a large flatscreen television, a large-print Bible, an enormous digital clock, a magnetic monthly calendar that took up half the refrigerator door. She noticed a magnifying glass near the reading chair, and by the door stood a white cane often used by the blind.

A balding, middle-aged man was sitting by himself in the living room idly browsing the day-old paper, while in the bathroom an elderly woman was busy applying the last of her makeup.

"Thank you for driving me," the woman said through the open door as she fussed with her hair. Though her voice and mannerisms appeared familiar, Julia was certain that they had never met before.

"That's what family is for," the man said with a smile. "Just remember that I'm the good child who gave you a ride when my sisters wouldn't."

"Couldn't," she corrected with a laugh. "After all, they're busy cooking us Christmas dinner."

"Still, I'm the one risking life and limb in this weather. Surely that entitles me to extra bonus points."

"Afraid not, dear. But perhaps you could have an extra slice or two of the birthday cake. Don't forget to bring it with us!"

"I won't," the man assured her as he patted the cake pan next to him. "And even if it doesn't make me your favorite child, I'm thankful for the opportunity to chauffeur you around. I know it was hard, but I'm glad you gave up driving for good."

His mother sighed. "I am too, though I miss the independence. But I am too much of a risk to myself and others with only half my eyesight. I hope the cake turned out okay. Somedays I can't even see well enough to make instant coffee in the morning."

As the woman turned off the bathroom light and walked toward the front door, Julia saw her face for the first time and instantly recognized her.   Mary. Her long-suffering secretary whose husband Julia had made unemployed.   Looking at the man more closely, she recognized him as Mary's eldest child who was so angry at her for causing their misfortunate.

"You know," the son said as knelt before his mother to help her put on her boots, "you are always welcome to live with my wife and I now that father has passed away.   With the kids off to college, we have plenty of room and would welcome the company."

"I know, Jacob, and thank you for the offer," she replied as silent tears leaked from her eyes. "Maybe by next Christmas I will have to.   But for now, I want to stay as independent as I can."

Julia looked at the phantom with fear in her questioning eyes.   Why, she wondered, could Mary no longer drive or even live on her own?

She has macular degeneration, came the explanation.   *She was being treated successfully with shots in her eyes, but Medicare stopped paying for them because they were too expensive. Now, very little can be done to slow her steady decline into blindness.*

Rationing of medical care?   Once the wealthiest country in the world, her government now had no choice but to cut costs by letting senior citizens go blind because it had ran out of other people's money. Julia slowly shook her head in amazement that she had ever thought government-run health care was a good idea. How was it that the people who ran the department of motor vehicles were put in charge of people's health care decisions?

You voted for it. You advocated it. In fact, you were one of the most vigorous proponents of rationing Medicare in order to "preserve access for everyone." You even sat behind the president as he signed the bill into law, and now a new signing pen graces your wall.

Julia's face lost its color as she realized that she had not only caused Mary such misery, but that similar scenes to this one were being repeated throughout the country because of her. Rather than advocate that the government should extradite itself from the health insurance industry it only made worse, she had encouraged it on the road to bankruptcy and cost rationing.

"Maybe you could ask Julia to pay for your shots," Jacob said with a bitter laugh. "I heard Medicare recently paid for her plastic surgery. She now looks ten years younger, though she can't smile because her face is stretched too tight. But come to think of it, she hardly smiled even when she was able to."

"I tried to ask her," Mary quietly admitted to her son's amazement, "but she refused to answer the door. I saw her briefly in her bedroom window, but then she took a sip from the bottle in her hand and went back to her drunken stupor."

Julia stood there weeping, horrified at the realization that her unfulfilled narcissism had driven her future self to such despondency that she would close the door on one of the few friends in life she actually had. She suddenly remembered Mary's words from the earlier vision: *"Selfishness blinds many people."* Mary, she realized, would see more blind than Julia had ever seen with sight.

"Drunken egomaniac," Jacob said as he helped Mary with her coat. "I wish she couldn't hide from her victims behind a veil of drunkenness."

"She'll have all eternity to be haunted by them, though I still hold out hope that she might find redemption," Mary replied with cautious optimism, closing the door behind them as they left to spend Christmas with their family.

Julia cried with such force that it took her breath away, overcome by Mary's undeserved love despite all she had done to her. After tonight, she vowed, she will endeavor to love Mary more than herself. And her family as well, even if her husband and children do not return it.

Genuine love, Julia realized, is sacrificially giving without any expectation of reciprocity. She recalled the words of the beggar from earlier in the day: *"Love does not boast, it is not proud, it is not self-seeking."* Love, she finally understood, is the humble pouring out of one's life in a selfless desire to serve others, regardless of whether anyone ever knows or acknowledges it.

The dark mist once again surrounded them as the scythe struck the floor, and as it receded Julia saw that they were standing several hundred feet from a graveyard service. Paralyzed with fear, Julia knew instinctively that she was watching her own funeral.

The phantom stopped and looked back at her. *This story does not have to be written*, he reminded her. *You, and only you, have the power to change your future.*

The Spirit's unheard words startled her with their simplicity. She alone held the key to her release from the chain of selfishness with which she had imprisoned herself. It was only by dying to herself that she would ever truly be alive, free from the bondage of fear and guilt.

Strangely, Julia no longer felt any anxiety as they walked between rows upon rows of those who had preceded her in death. She no longer feared the inevitability of the grave, for this was her night of redemption. She would soon be buried here herself, but not before she could repent of her sins and make restitution.

As they approached the service, Julia counted only a handful of people gathered around her casket. Mary, with genuine sorrow etched in her face, was there as the sole representative of her family. She was dutifully flanked by two other employees of Julia's company, both of whom looked to be there more for Mary's sake than for Julia's.

The other two attendees were the funeral home director and the pastor he hired to say a few words for the deceased. Kind words were not specified, nor were they given. Instead, the pastor described in excruciating detail the emptiness of Julia's life of selfishness, and exhorted his listeners to flee from it in favor of a life of joyful sacrifice.

Julia was neither surprised by the meager attendance nor the fact that the service wasn't held in an actual church. She had had no use for God since the government provided for her daily bread. Nor did she ever marry because the government took care of and protected her. And she never cared for anyone else, because that was the government's job.

And in the end she died alone, without even a token representative from her self-made god of government to mourn her passing. Her demise was perfunctorily noted by an army of bureaucrats as they removed her name from the government entitlement roles, but not a single one bothered to shed a tear or send a card. She was simply just another impersonal number that was worth more to the government dead than alive.

"Bah humbug!" Julia yelled at the empty illusion of her self-made god, punctuating the sentiment by spitting on the ground. But as she once more looked at the faces of her mourners, she realized in horror the full extent of the delusion of her own life. Zachary wasn't present.

She had adopted a son solely to ensure her fond remembrance upon her death, and now he wasn't even present for her funeral. He was likely too busy playing violent video games or, worse yet, playing out their savagery in real life. Her only legacy in this world was how she influenced others, and all she had to show for it was a chain full of victims. The most prominent of which was her only child.

Her life was nothing more than a humbug. A fiction. A lie. The only thing real about it was the pain she caused others. She had strived to create a glittering image of herself, but underneath the facade was a very empty and cruel person. She had sacrificed everything good in her life on the altar of her own self-aggrandizement.

In the end, she grudgingly admitted to herself, she was her own self-made god. She had idolized government not for its own sake, but for her's instead. She had worshiped it because it was an enabler, a means to a consequence-free utopia of worldly pleasures. Like any druggie to its supplier, her loyalty to the government would end as soon as it stopped providing for her unquenchable greed. It, as with everything else in her life, was a tool of her narcissism.

As Julia saw the cemetery workers slowly lower her casket into the ground, she saw with surprise that her grave was already marked with a life-size monument of herself. She was standing gallantly with feet square against the world, one hand holding a parchment version of Julia's Law while the other pointed forward as if leading the world to a better future.

The plaque read: "Here lies Julia. Champion for a better tomorrow." It then catalogued all the laws that she had helped pass, giving special place of honor to Julia's Law and the Medicare rationing bill. Julia wept as she gazed at the hundreds of statutes she had had a hand in passing, cringing at the thought of the countless victims each bill had created. This was her better future, a world in which everyone lived at the expense of somebody else.

With alarm, Julia noticed that missing from the otherwise magnificent monument was its head, which was no where to be found. Instead, in its place the villain had mounted a taxidermic pig with money oozing out of both ends. Before leaving, the culprit had crudely spray painted the monument with a simple message: "I hate you, Mom!"

"No!" Julia shouted as she ran to the monument in a frantic attempt to scrub away the hateful words. But her hands, unable to break the barrier of time, merely brushed the air in a futile effort to connect with the marble surface. Defeated, Julia fell to her knees in uncontrollable grief, overcome with sorrow at the monster she helped create.

Zachary has yet to be born, the Spirit sought to comfort her. *This does not have to be either your fate or his*.

"And what is his fate?" Julia asked with a growing sense of foreboding. "What happens to Zachary?"

The phantom, appearing to hesitate for just a second as sorrow briefly emanated from his pale, lantern-like eyes, quickly buried them in a cloud of black mist as his scythe once more hit the ground. As the fog retreated, Julia anxiously saw that they remained at her gravesite.

The unrestored monument, now weathered with time, stood as a stark reminder of the vanity of pride. The pig, though a little worse for the wear, nonetheless still sat snugly on the shoulders, its currency long since replaced by Monopoly money. The ground before it, overrun with grass badly in need of a trim, showed no signs of the hole they had once dug.

But next to her plot two workers were busy excavating a final resting place for a recent arrival who awaited in the hearse. The grave was already marked by a simple tombstone that read: "Zachary. Son of Julia. Killer."

"Why don't they make them dig their own graves before they execute them?" the chubby worker complained as he wiped the sweat from his brow.

"Because that would be cruel and unusual punishment," his taller companion replied with a laugh. "Besides, at least we're getting paid to do it."

"Still, a monster like him doesn't deserve his own grave. His death was too kind for what he had done, and now his grave will become a shrine to the next generation of would-be serial killers."

Horrified as she heard the term *serial killer*, Julia desperately threw herself at the base of her statue as she sought unsuccessfully to close her senses to the scene before her.

Nodding his head in agreement, the taller man recounted the death toll, "Eleven confirmed deaths. All of them successful, beautiful, single-mothers who were tortured to death."

"It's no mystery who inspired him," the hearse driver chimed in with a droll chuckle as he gave a slight nod towards Julia's grave.

"Did you notice that the papers never mentioned who his mother was?" the fat man asked. "She was always called 'his mother.' Never had a name. Never once were her supposed contributions to society mentioned. She was just a mother to a monster."

"Now she's just a nobody," the driver agreed. "Just another self-righteous fool who won't even make it as a footnote in the history books."

Julia wished the Spirit had never shown her this final vision. Nothing that she had treasured in this life had actually mattered. She had lived for her own glory, and now none of her achievements had outlived her. The only thing that still testified to her life was her decapitated and defaced shrine to her own vanity.

"She's lucky she wasn't one of his victims, though her statue didn't fare as well," the tall man said as he flung a clump of dirt at the marble gravestone. "They found the head in his bedroom when they arrested him, smashed to such fine dust it was almost unrecognizable."

"Arrested for social security fraud," the driver added. "Caught still cashing his mother's social security checks five years after her death."

"The egomaniac thought they had finally come to arrest him for the murders and confessed on the spot," the tall man scoffed. "What a fool. Turns out that nothing in the house tied him to the deaths. He was convicted by his own boastful words."

Nodding at the hearse, the fat man concurred, "He was an arrogant butcher. Learned it from his mother. He spent his entire interview mocking the detectives for not arresting him sooner."

"And then at the trial he pled guilty by reason of insanity," the tall man said with exacerbation. "Their expert testified that he had been driven insane by his mother. Thank goodness the jury didn't buy it."

"They had the video of his confession in which he described how he had intentionally tortured and mutilated the victims," the driver explained. "He even admitted that he knew it was wrong."

"No, he said he knew society believed it was wrong," the fat man corrected. "He proudly informed the police that anything he did for his own gratification was morally acceptable."

"Still," the driver persisted, "the jury only took five minutes to convict him of all eleven murders and sentence him to death."

"And the egomaniac just laughed at them and proclaimed he couldn't be killed," the tall man snickered. "Now the jury is having the last laugh."

With that the three men collapsed into convulsions of laughter at the arrogance of selfishness.

Julia stood there horrified at the demon she had helped create. Zachary, a jury had rightfully determined, was clearly responsible for his own actions. While his past may have shaped him, it did not control him. He had made the decision of his own free will to become the embodiment of unbridled evil—choosing to embrace his own selfishness without regard for any moral or societal restraints.

Still, he had inherited such nihilistic egotism from her, learning to judge morality not by any objective measure but by what brought him the most pleasure. She had kept her narcissism in check out of concern for what others might think of her, but he had no similar qualms.

He had believed himself a god, and the world his playground. The only limit on his power was its finiteness. Not being God, he eventually discovered that there were others more powerful than he was.

No, Julia sadly concluded, she wasn't the mother of a monster. She was a monster who had begot a monster.

As she turned with tear-stained cheeks to beg the Spirit to take her home, she saw the scene around her suddenly collapse into the black mist as her bedroom once more materialized before her.

STAVE FIVE.

THE END OF IT

Julia found herself hugging the leg of her bed where just moments before she had sought refuge at the base of her monument. Overcome with relief that her night of redemption was now complete, she prayerfully knelt in profound gratitude at the opportunity she had been given for repentance and reformation.

Slowly rising to her feet, Julia noticed that the fireplace poker remained embedded in the bedroom wall where she had hurled it. Embarrassed at her foolish fright, she tried in vain to pull it free from the wall that obstinately refused to release it from its grasp. Sighing in resignation, she decided to leave it as a memorial to this night of grace she had not deserved.

Suddenly the bells began to toll as they welcomed in a new hour, causing Julia's heart to freeze in panic at the thought of being visited by more supernatural visions of her victims. But unlike before, she heard only the bells from the nearby church ringing as they welcomed in Christ's birthday.

As the twelfth chime faded into the night, Julia realized in bewilderment that she had somehow gone back in time to the moment of the first spirit's arrival. Thinking that he might have felt the need for an encore presentation, Julia rushed to the window to graciously but firmly decline the performance.

But rather than a specter, Julia was greeted by the sight of families strolling in solemn remembrance down her street.

Puzzled, she pushed open her window and cried out, "Where are you going?"

"To the midnight service," a father replied after recovering from his surprise at the unexpected voice coming from above.

With a start, Julia remembered that the church maintained a midnight Christmas service when all other churches in town had moved their services, if they had any at all, to more convenient times. The church stubbornly refused to change with contemporary sensibilities, noting that Jesus had been born at night after Mary and Joseph had traveled all day.

"I'll be there soon!" Julia shouted as she whirled back to her bedroom in search of some clothes.

Five minutes later, a disheveled but very radiant Julia found herself sitting in a church pew for the first time in decades. After the children's choir finished singing *Away in the Manger*, the pastor read the Christmas story and offered communion to the overflowing congregation.

Then as the lights were being dimmed and the candles passed out, she saw with embarrassment that she was sitting near the carolers she had treated so rudely earlier in the evening. Though fearing rejection, Julia summoned the courage to whisper a tearful apology to the group as everyone stood for the candlelight service.

Rather than ostracism and mockery, the woman closest to her gave her a warm embrace while several others engulfed her small hand in their firm handshakes. Shocked by the miracle of forgiveness, Julia stood there amazed that through an act of humility she had now made new friends. She had just created a stronger bond with these recent strangers than she would ever have with a government charity worker.

As they joined together in singing *Silent Night*, Julia reminded herself that her night of redemption wasn't entirely complete. There can be no redemption without repentance, and there can be no repentance without first apologizing and making amends. The final leg of her arduous journey had yet to be taken.

After they had sung several more hymns and the service concluded, Julia stayed to meet the carolers and invite them to her house for dinner the following weekend. Laughing with joy, they enthusiastically accepted her invitation with promises to bring side dishes and games.

Walking home, Julia at last begun to feel a measure of peace as several of the links fell off her chain. Instead of ignoring her guilt over her treatment of the carolers, she had repented of her behavior and found redemption. And now, for the first time in her adult life, she was experiencing the fruit of that redemption—the peace that comes from having a clean conscience.

Having no desire to sleep even if she could, Julia spent the early hours of Christmas morning plotting to purge the last of her guilt. She would spend the day seeking forgiveness from those in town she knew: Mary and her family, her former employer, and the bell ringer from earlier this evening.

She thought of the desperate beggar whom she had yelled at as she left the cemetery on her way to work. She had no idea of his name or where he lived, but promised herself that she would find him to apologize and help his family in any way she could.

The visions she saw tonight did not reveal all of her victims, and those it did show were largely images of nameless misery. But she knew the names of two of her victims: Fred, the leukemia survivor, and Brad, her high school valedictorian.

She briefly toyed with the idea of simply sending them letters of apology, but quickly concluded that repentance should be done in person if possible. Impersonal modes of communication were only a means of hiding from her victims, a veil by which she could escape viewing the pain she had caused. As with the carolers in the church, she had to be willing to risk shame, rejection, and ridicule on her journey of repentance.

Perhaps the only restitution she could offer them, or any of her countless victims, would be a life lived at her expense rather than of taxpayers. She vowed to accept neither Social Security nor Medicare upon retirement, pledging to make enough to survive with the fruit of her own labor rather that of somebody else's. Finding her social security card, she tore it up and mailed it to the government with the words "social security swindle" emblazoned on the envelope.

She also penned a letter requesting the government to tax her at the normal sales and corporate income tax rates, and enclosed an initial installment for repaying both her mortgage bailout and student grants. Tearing up her government business loan agreement, Julia made a note to herself to visit her banker the next day to refinance it with a private one.

In addition to making amends, Julia realized that she had to publicly apologize for her efforts to live off of the labor of others. Her legions of nameless victims may never appreciate or even notice her apology, but hopefully her story of redemption will help end the modern slavocratic regime of wealth redistribution.

When morning finally arrived, Julia enjoyed a quick shower and hasty breakfast before leaving her house in search of her victims. Dropping the letters in the post office drop box, Julia's step became light, even joyful, as the crushing weight of her chain was gradually replaced by an all-encompassing sense of peace.

Pausing only briefly in hesitation, Julia overcame her fears and firmly knocked at the home of the president of her former company. She could hear cries of happy children in the background as they tore through their presents, and the smell of bacon and eggs wafted tantalizingly in the air to great her.

The door finally opened to reveal a plump, pajama-clad executive with a jolly face that quickly soured at the sight of Julia on his doorstep. He held a piece of bacon in one hand, while with the other he sipped coffee out of a mug inscribed with the words "World's Best Dad" on it's side.

"What do you want?" he said gruffly as he partially closed the door in an attempt to discourage her.

"I've come to apologize," she replied with tear-filled eyes as she boldly blocked the door from closing with her foot.

Staring at her in skeptical disbelief, he attempted to shut the door completely while muttering, "It's a little late for that, don't you think?"

"No, because I'm returning the jury verdict. All of it," Julia said as peace flooded her soul. "And I want you to hire back every single worker you had to lay off."

Staring at her in amazement, the president nearly dropped his cup of coffee before recovering his senses. Finding himself as a lose for words, he shoved the last of the bacon in his mouth in hopes that somehow its deliciousness would restore his powers of speech.

"And I want you to inform the workers today so that they can have a very merry Christmas," Julia continued, surprised by the ease with which she had begun to use the word *Christmas*. "But please don't tell Mary's husband yet. I want to do that in person later today."

Still speechless, the executive gulped from his now lukewarm coffee in an effort to find something for his gaping mouth to do other than futilely attempt to form words.

"Will you be available for a press conference at noon tomorrow?" Julia asked the still befuddled man. "I will meet with my attorney in the morning to sign and file the paperwork, and I want to hold a press conference afterwards. Not to boast over my change of heart, but to tell the world how black my heart was and to lobby for a repeal of the Lilly Ledbetter Act."

"I, um, yes, ah...that would be fine," the poor man finally managed.

As she turned to continue her journey, the executive, suddenly finding his voice, profusely thanked her and wished her a blessed Christmas.

Smiling at the relief she felt, Julia made her way to the homeless shelter with peace in her heart and hope in her step. Few staff members were present at this early hour, and nobody noticed as Julia slipped an envelope of bills into the entryway donation box.

Walking the halls in search of a volunteer coordinator, Julia's quest was interrupted by a chuckle and a booming "Merry Christmas!"

Turning to find the source of the voice, Julia found herself face-to-face with the bell ringer from last night.

"And what are you doing here?" he asked with laughter in his eyes.

Now it was her turn to be flustered. "I, huh, I'm here to...I would like to volunteer," she eventually sputtered.

It wasn't like her to be so shy, but she was struck by both his name tag and his looks. The forty year old man appeared far more handsome in daylight than she had remembered, and the name Benjamin was proudly displayed on his tag, followed by the title of executive director.

"But why should you volunteer for something that isn't needed?" he gently chided. "Wouldn't it be better if everyone's resources were given to government charity programs?"

"I was a fool, blinded by my own selfishness," she willingly admitted. Then, quoting his own words from earlier in the evening, she added, "'Government charity is coerced charity. It is no charity at all, but simply robbery sanctioned by the law.' And I'm tired of being a robber."

"We would be delighted to serve along side you," he said with a smile. "Would you be able to help serve today's Christmas dinner?"

"I already have plans for dinner, but I would be happy to help clean up later this afternoon."

"Great! Just head to the cafeteria at the end of the hall up there, and we'll put you to work," he grinned.

"Sounds good," Julia replied as she turned to go. She found herself bewitched by that smile, and the caring, blue eyes that were incapable of holding a grudge. She was surprised at herself, unable to recall the last time she allowed herself to indulge in feelings of romantic attraction.

"Wait!" Benjamin called, "I didn't catch your name."

"Julia," she replied as she paused to look at his slightly reddening face.

"Julia. What a beautiful name," he said somewhat bashfully. "Would you care to join me for dinner Friday night?"

"I would be honored," she replied without hesitation, her checks quickly flushing to match his.

Leaving after finalizing their date, Julia felt tears welling up in her eyes. Tears of happiness after so many of sorrow were shed the night before. She felt alive like she hadn't in years, overcome with joy at being able to love and be loved in return.

Maybe, Julia thought, it wasn't too late for her to find a husband and start a family. But, if marriage wasn't in her future, she promised herself that she would have children someday. Not for her own vanity, but out of a genuine desire to leave the world with a legacy of love.

And she would adopt children in need, not some designer child picked out of a magazine. Perhaps she'll adopt twin boys from Africa who have been diagnosed with HIV. Or possibly an entire set of siblings suffering under the oppression of a distant dictator. Or maybe a child born here at home with cerebral palsy or down syndrome.

Smiling as she considered the prospect of both adopting and having children of her own, Julia hurried home to take a quick nap and make a fruit salad for dinner at Mary's.

An hour later, refreshed and reenergized, Julia arrived at Mary's home with desert in her hand and joy in her heart. If peace is the fruit of redemption, she realized, than surely joy is the fruit of peace. Only those who have had their guilt replaced by soul-cleansing peace can experience such a joy unspeakable.

Pausing as she saw the "for sale" sign, Julia impulsively pulled it out of the ground and placed it by the trash can on the far side of the house. She'll replace it if they want to move, but she had no intention of seeing them exiled because of her actions.

"Merry Christmas!" she cried as Mary opened the door, giving especial emphasis to the word *Christ*.

Quickly recovering from her surprise, Mary threw open the door and gave Julia a tearful embrace. Together the two of them cried tears of happiness, Julia at the surprise of joy and Mary at its transformation.

"I brought you some salad," Julia said when at last they parted.

"You didn't have to do that," Mary replied. "Dinner should be here soon."

"I wanted to. I—," Julia paused as she saw Jacob and Mary's husband watching with smoldering bitterness. "I now know the harm I have caused your family, and I wanted to seek your forgiveness."

The anger melting with each step he took, Mary's husband engulfed her in a giant bear hug with the whispered words, "I forgive you, Julia."

"I just talked with your boss and you will be starting work tomorrow," she told him once she could breathe again. "They are rehiring all of the laid off workers."

"But how?" he sputtered in disbelief, amazed at the blessings of Providence.

"I've returned the money," she said simply, "and I will work to overturn the law."

Giving her another hug, Mary rejoiced, "You once were blind, but now you see."

"My heart was hardened by selfishness," Julia confessed, "but now I have found redemption."

Seeing Jacob joined by his sisters, she apologized for not bringing them any presents.

"You have brought us more than enough," Jacob assured her with a smile. "Dad now has his job back, and we don't have to move."

"I hope you don't mind that I put the 'for sale' sign in the trash," she said as she gave an envelope to his father. "And here's a little something to tie you over until your first paycheck."

"Please, I can't accept this," he protested.

"It's the least that I can do," she insisted. "I can't pay back the wages you and your co-workers lost, but at least I can make a downpayment. Repentance, after all, requires some form of restitution."

Leaving their house several hours later to return to the shelter, Julia smiled as she found herself singing the lines of the Christmas carol they had sung before dessert: *Happy Birthday, Jesus*!

APPENDIX

During the 2012 U.S. presidential election, the Obama campaign released the following sketch of a fictional character named Julia on which this novel is loosely based. This book is not intended to be a partisan pamphlet against Democrats or for Republicans.

Rather, it opposes any use of the law, regardless of the party advocating it, to take from one person what belongs to them in order to give it to others to whom it does not belong. Because it has no money of its own, the government cannot perform an act of charity without first stealing from someone else. It cannot help some without sacrificing others on the altar of electoral greed.

OBAMA'S LIFE OF JULIA

1. As a child, Julia is enrolled in a Head Start program to help get her ready for school.

2. Julia takes the SAT and is on track to start her college applications. Her high school is part of the Race to the Top program, and their new college-and-career-ready standards mean Julia can take the classes she needs to do well.

3. As she prepares for her first semester of college, Julia and her family qualify for the American Opportunity Tax Credit—worth up to

$10,000 over four years. Julia is also one of millions of students who receive a Pell Grant to help put a college education within reach.

4. During college, Julia undergoes surgery. It is thankfully covered by her insurance due to a provision in ObamaCare that lets her stay on her parents' coverage until she turns 26.

5. Because of steps like the Lilly Ledbetter Fair Pay Act, Julia is one of millions of women across the country who knows she'll always be able to stand up for her right to equal pay. She starts her career as a web designer.

6. After graduation, Julia's federal student loans are more manageable since the government capped income-based federal student loan payments and kept interest rates low.

7.   For the past four years, Julia has worked full-time as a web designer. Thanks to Obamacare, her health insurance is required to cover birth control and preventive care, letting Julia focus on her work rather than worry about her health.

8. Julia decides to have a child. Throughout her pregnancy, she benefits from maternal checkups, prenatal care, and free screenings under health care reform.

9. Julia's son Zachary starts kindergarten. The public schools in their neighborhood have better facilities and great teachers because of government spending in education and programs like Race to the Top.

10.   Julia starts her own web business.   She qualifies for a Small Business Administration loan, giving her the money she needs to invest in her business. Tax cuts for small businesses like Julia's help her get started. She's able to hire employees, create new jobs in her town, and help to grow the local economy.

11.   Julia enrolls in Medicare, helping her to afford preventive care and the prescription drugs she needs.

12.   Julia retires. After years of contributing to Social Security, she receives monthly benefits that help her retire comfortably, without worrying that she'll run out of savings. This allows her to volunteer at a community garden.

NATHAN W. TUCKER

Nathan Tucker is an author and attorney who lives in Iowa. He has been a regular columnist for The Iowa Republican and the Tea Party Tribune, as well as a guest columnist for a number of media outlets.

He has a prior novel—*Letters from Cell No. 73*— as well as two nonfiction books: *Constitutional Musings: An Anthology of Legal Columns* and *We the People: The Only Cure to Judicial Activism*.